A MIDLIFE CATASTROPHE

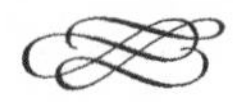

MORGANA BEST

A Midlife CatAstrophe
MenoPaws Mysteries Book 1

ISBN 9781922595058

GLOSSARY

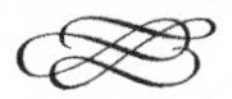

Some Australian spellings and expressions are entirely different from US spellings and expressions. Below are just a few examples.

It would take an entire book to list all the differences.

For example, people often think "How are you going?" (instead of "How are you doing?") is an error, but it's normal and correct for Aussies!

The author has used Australian spelling in this series. Here are a few examples: *Mum* instead of the US spelling *Mom*, *neighbour* instead of the US spelling *neighbor*, *fulfil* instead of *fulfill*, *realise* instead of the US spelling *realize*. It is *Ms*, *Mr* and *Mrs* in Australia, not *Ms.*, *Mr.* and *Mrs.*; *defence* not *defense; judgement* not *judgment; cosy* and not *cozy; 1930s* not *1930's*; *offence* not *offense*; *centre* not *center*; *towards* not *toward*; *jewellery* not *jewelry*; *favour* not *favor*; *mould* not *mold*; *two storey house* not *two story house*; *practise* (verb) not *practice* (verb); *odour* not *odor*; *smelt* not *smelled*; *travelling* not *traveling; liquorice* not *licorice; cheque not check; leant* not *leaned; have concussion* not *have a concussion; anti clockwise* not *counterclockwise; go to hospital* not *go to the hospital; sceptic* not *skeptic; aluminium* not *aluminum; learnt* not *learned*. We have *fancy dress* parties not *costume* parties. We don't say *gotten*. We say *car crash* (or *accident*) not *car wreck*. We say *a herb* not *an herb* as we pronounce the 'h.'

The above are just a few examples.

It's not just different words; Aussies sometimes use different expressions in sentence structure. We might *eat a curry* not *eat curry*. We might say *in the main street* not *on the main street*. Someone might be *going well* instead of *doing well*. We might say *without drawing breath* not *without drawing a breath*.

These are just some of the differences.

Please note that these are not mistakes or typos, but correct, normal Aussie spelling, terms, and syntax.

AUSTRALIAN SLANG AND TERMS

Benchtops - counter tops (kitchen)
Big Smoke - a city
Blighter - infuriating or good-for-nothing person
Blimey! - an expression of surprise
Bloke - a man (usually used in nice sense, "a good bloke")
Blue (noun) - an argument ("to have a blue")
Bluestone - copper sulphate (copper sulfate in US spelling)
Bluo - a blue laundry additive, an optical brightener
Boot (car) - trunk (car)
Bonnet (car) - hood (car)
Bore - a drilled water well
Budgie smugglers (variant: budgy smugglers) - named after the Aussie native bird, the budgerigar. A slang term for brief and tight-fitting men's swimwear
Bugger! - as an expression of surprise, not a swear word
Bugger - as in "the poor bugger" - refers to an unfortunate person (not a swear word)
Bunging it on - faking something, pretending

Bush telegraph - the grapevine, the way news spreads by word of mouth in the country
Car park - parking lot
Cark it - die
Chooks - chickens
Come good - turn out okay
Copper, cop - police officer
Coot - silly or annoying person
Cream bun - a sweet bread roll with copious amounts of cream, plus jam (= jelly in US) in the centre
Crook - 1. "Go crook (on someone)" - to berate them. 2. (someone is) crook - (someone is) ill. 3. Crook (noun) - a criminal
Demister (in car) - defroster
Drongo - an idiot
Dunny - an outhouse, a toilet, often ramshackle
Fair crack of the whip - a request to be fair, reasonable, just
Flannelette (fabric) - cotton, wool, or synthetic fabric, one side of which has a soft finish.
Flat out like a lizard drinking water - very busy
Galah - an idiot
Garbage - trash
G'day - Hello
Give a lift (to someone) - give a ride (to someone)

Goosebumps - goose pimples
Gumboots - rubber boots, wellingtons
Knickers - women's underwear
Laundry (referring to the room) - laundry room
Lamingtons - iconic Aussie cakes, square, sponge, chocolate-dipped, and coated with desiccated coconut. Some have a layer of cream and strawberry jam (= jelly in US) between the two halves.
Lift - elevator
Like a stunned mullet - very surprised
Mad as a cut snake - either insane or very angry
Mallee bull (as fit as, as mad as) - angry and/or fit, robust, super strong.
Miles - while Australians have kilometres these days, it is common to use expressions such as, "The road stretched for miles," "It was miles away."
Moleskins - woven heavy cotton fabric with suede-like finish, commonly used as working wear, or as town clothes
Mow (grass / lawn) - cut (grass / lawn)
Neenish tarts - Aussie tart. Pastry base. Filling is based on sweetened condensed milk mixture or mock cream. Some have layer of raspberry jam (jam = jelly in US). Topping is in two equal

halves: icing (= frosting in US), usually chocolate on one side, and either lemon or pink on the other.
Pub - The pub at the south of a small town is often referred to as the 'bottom pub' and the pub at the north end of town, the 'top pub.' The size of a small town is often judged by the number of pubs - i.e. "It's a three pub town."
Red cattle dog - (variant: blue cattle dog usually known as a 'blue dog') - referring to the breed of Australian Cattle Dog. However, a 'red dog' is usually a red kelpie (another breed of dog)
Shoot through - leave
Shout (a drink) - to buy a drink for someone
Skull (a drink) - drink a whole drink without stopping
Stone the crows! - an expression of surprise
Takeaway (food) - Take Out (food)
Toilet - also refers to the room if it is separate from the bathroom
Torch - flashlight
Tuck in (to food) - to eat food hungrily
Ute /Utility - pickup truck
Vegemite - Australian food spread, thick, dark brown
Wardrobe - closet

Windscreen - windshield

Indigenous References

Bush tucker - food that occurs in the Australian bush

Koori - the original inhabitants/traditional custodians of the land of Australia in NSW. *Murri* are the people just to the north. White European culture often uses the term, *Aboriginal people.*

ABOUT

When Nell Darling moves to a small Aussie mountain town after a messy divorce, she decides her life will be purrfect. But life has decided to be no such thing. Nell discovers a body, buys a mysterious bookstore, and starts to suspect she is losing her mind--all because a local cat begins stopping by for a chat.

Yet Nell has no time to paws and reflect. Soon she is chasing her tail to solve the murder. Hot on her heels is the dreamy Detective Caspian Cole, who seems to think Nell is mad fur real. But it doesn't matter what Detective Cole thinks, because Nell is about to discover that menopause doesn't mean her life is put on pause.

In fact, menopause is a sign that Nell's has finally begun.

Litter-ally a fun read for women who are coming into their power!

CHAPTER 1

Twenty-one. I owned sweaters older than my husband's mistress. What's more, I couldn't even feel angry with the glorified child, because the girl wasn't even my husband's *only* mistress. Imagine that, Jack Darling, a man with more fudge in his stomach than stomach, a man with thinning hair, a red, bulbous nose, and pink, plump cheeks had managed to entice *multiple* women, and they were not even blind.

The other day at the car yard, a man a decade older than I am hadn't so much as stolen a look at my legs. No, he was too busy salivating over the secretary, who was around twenty, trim, and perky. Not that men looked at me anymore. Why is it, I wondered, as I drummed my fingers against the steering wheel, that my husband hadn't wanted me to be desirable?

I had wanted to be desirable. I hadn't wanted my husband of twenty-three years to lust after every woman who glittered in front of him. My husband did not like me being glittery. He liked me wearing good, sensible shoes. He complained when I covered my greys. He liked me to wear dungarees, which was all the fashion with the toddlers on my street.

My *old* street.

I turned up my car's air-conditioning. I couldn't tell if it was another menopausal hot flash or anger, but I supposed it didn't matter, really. A flash was a flash.

I'd pretended to like so many stupid things in order to please Jack. Like hiking. I was not a hiker. I didn't even like hiking boots, which our daughter wore so well. And what about camping? Who likes camping? Why leave a perfectly good house with four walls and a roof and a screen door that stops mosquitos to go to the bathroom in the bushland with venomous snakes lurking nearby?

It's because men have it too easy, I realised. They don't have to battle pregnancy or getting paid less than their contemporaries for doing the same job. That is why men needed to make life difficult for themselves.

My phone buzzed. "Hello," I said, speaking loudly so my daughter could hear.

"Mum, are you at Wild Lime Mountain yet?"

It was hard to hear over the air-conditioning. "What?"

"The mountain?" Eliza yelled.

"Not yet."

Wild Lime Mountain. The place of my escape. My new life.

"Call me when you arrive," Eliza replied and hung up.

I sniffled. I'd never in a million years seen the divorce coming. How is it that you can plan a life for yourself and commit to that life for twenty-three years, and then, when your husband couldn't take another day with the woman who stood by him as he built himself up from nothing, you end up homeless and without a husband? Didn't I get a say? Didn't my voice count for anything? No, apparently not.

Not when Jack had taken out a mortgage on our house without my knowledge. Not when Jack had a *five-year-old* child with his mistress of *ten years*.

Ten years ago, I was crying in the car because I'd found cigarettes in Eliza's schoolbag. Meanwhile, my husband was brushing legs with somebody at work.

Eliza once told me, "Mum, men fall out of love more quickly than women."

But I knew that wasn't true. Often men have the money, which means they have the power to leave. They are not dependent on their wives because their wives gave up everything to support their husband's dream. I could never have left that marriage. I was the homemaker. I didn't care about the degrading things people said about staying at home. To me, raising my child was more important than working to line the pockets of an already well-lined pocket so that other people could raise their children. Not that I judged working mothers. No, I admired them, the way I admired all women. Jack had agreed I should stay at home.

But what happens when a homemaker is no longer a homemaker? What happens when a woman who raised a child and kept a house no longer has a husband and therefore no longer has a breadwinner? What about the gaps in my resume? No one wanted to employ me, and I could no longer rely on Jack to help. How could a man take pride in himself as a man after he has thrown out the mother of his child?

I shook my head. It is probably why men like having multiple women, so if they fail at being a husband to one, they can simply knock on another door and give it a second try. I had no such luxury.

It was the fortune teller at the markets who had given me the solution. It had been another terrible week. I had a meeting at the job agency, where the twenty-something-year-old spoke in a loud, clear voice as if I were an idiot. He'd explained how the Internet worked—the Internet!—and had asked condescending questions about my reading abilities. He'd snorted when I said I'd chosen to stay at home and raise my daughter. He'd patted my hand condescendingly when I told him I was a quick learner. These people seemed to think that everyone without a job was stupid, but then maybe I *was* stupid. After all, I had not seen the divorce coming.

"How about a free reading?" the fortune teller had called as I walked through the markets. I had not wanted to talk to anyone. No, I'd wanted to buy organic bananas and local jam in peace before scurrying back to my car, where I planned to eat dark chocolate.

"I don't think so, sorry," I had replied. I knew how these fortune tellers worked. They offered a free reading, and when they had you hooked, they charged four hundred, even five hundred, dollars.

"I'm sorry about your husband," the fortune teller said then.

That staggered me.

"And I'm sorry you need to move."

"Move?" Now I was really shocked. "I'm not moving."

"Yes," the fortune teller replied. "You are. You are moving to Wild Lime Mountain."

Wild Lime Mountain? I'd heard of it, sure, a beautiful touristy town up north in Queensland, somewhere in the Gold Coast Hinterland. "Why on earth…"

"Because it is where you are going to buy a bookshop."

"I'm not going to buy a bookshop," I said, though I was very fond of books. "How could I possibly buy a bookshop?"

"Things are meant to find each other that do," the fortune teller had said.

And she was right, although more than

anything, it was a self-fulfilling prophecy. Five days later, I had bought a bookshop on Wild Lime Mountain. I wouldn't have looked at businesses for sale if the woman hadn't put the idea into my head, but I did, and there it was—a bookshop for sale in Wild Lime Mountain. The ad said the bookshop had a little apartment over it and added that Wild Lime Mountain was a welcoming community. I certainly hoped the ad was right. Maybe life would be different on Wild Lime Mountain.

Still, the price was right, a true shopping bargain, and the divorce settlement had left me sufficient money for the purchase and a little to spare.

I drew my attention back to the road. The road signs warned of steep mountains ahead, but they weren't as steep or as scary as the ones near where I used to live. Soon, I found myself at the top of the mountain and driving slowly along Lamington Lane, a straight road which was clearly the tourist centre of town. Cute little shops lined both sides of the street. I checked the GPS and kept driving.

I turned up the air conditioner in the car as a hot flash overwhelmed me. It felt as though my very insides were on fire. When it passed, I was shivering, so I turned the air-conditioner down once more.

A wave of apprehension washed over me. Had I done the right thing? Leaving my home and friends to go to another state where I knew not a soul, and what's more, buying a bookstore. I had never run a business, and I didn't know the first thing about it. I fought the urge to turn and run.

Now, after seven hours of driving, I was here, looking for my bookshop and a place to park.

I stepped out of my car and breathed in the crisp, clear mountain air. I turned around.

A man blocked my way. "You took my spot!" he screamed at me.

"I—what?" I replied.

"That was my parking spot." The man was short and pink and huffing and puffing, the way the wolf huffed and puffed to blow the little pig's house down. But I was not a little pig.

"You were nowhere near this spot when I parked here," I said, which was true. Besides, the car park was not even full. There were plenty of other places for the man to park.

The man's face turned a hideous shade of red. "I'll call the cops if you don't move your car!"

I was aware I was trembling. I didn't want to cry. I'd cried for half of the drive to this mountain, and I was tired of my eyes itching.

"Good." I hoped I sounded firm. "You call the police so I can have you arrested for harassing me."

The man made a show of removing his phone from his pocket, but before he could speak again, another man approached us. "What now?" I said aloud. Was this a little gang that went around harassing newcomers?

"Put your phone away, Rufus," said the second man. To me, he said, "I am Edison Chester." He bent forward in a half-bow. "You must be Nell Darling. Would you like a cup of tea?"

"No, I would certainly not," Rufus replied.

Edison chuckled. "Good, because I wasn't inviting you." He offered his arm to me. "I think you'll find your little shop quite charming."

Rufus called a few words after me that made my ears burn.

As I turned away, I was keenly aware that several people had stopped to watch this little altercation. If it weren't for Edison, I was almost certain hot tears would be falling down my face. Edison looked for all the world like a storybook wizard, complete with a shock of white hair and a shaggy white beard. Although he looked as old as the hills, he had a sprightly manner about him. A strange scent clung to him. I couldn't identify it, but I fancied it smelt like ancient herbs.

I looked down to see a fat ginger cat blocking my way. It was staring at me in such a way it unnerved me. Edison stepped around the cat and waved at the bookshop. I gasped with delight.

The façade was painted in hunter green, and the words, *A Likely Story*, were emblazoned in gold lettering over the top. All manner of books filled the wide bay window. I had seen photos of the building, but they hadn't done it justice. It looked like something one would see in the cobbled streets of Oxford, on the other side of the world.

The interior was lovely, warm and dusted and cosy, with faded armchairs next to green-shaded lamps and coasters on the windowsills which functioned as tables. I had bought the shop and my apartment fully furnished, and I was happy with the furniture, although it wasn't quite to my taste.

Edison led me to one of the armchairs. "Your books arrived yesterday. I had them taken upstairs to your apartment. They're all in the guest bedroom. I hope that was okay."

"That's great, thanks." I studied his face for disapproval but didn't find any signs. Of course, Edison loved books too. My ex-husband had condemned my passion for books, calling it obsessive. Edison's voice broke me out of my reverie.

"Lemongrass? Chamomile? I have a nice blend of cinnamon bark, cardamom seed, and ginger root. Or maybe a blend of liquorice root, slippery elm, wild cherry, and orange peel?"

I chose the latter for no particular reason. There I sat as he went to make me a cup of tea and also to attend to customers. The bookshop was not packed with people, but it was comfortably full, with a woman in owl-eyed spectacles pouring over a botany book to my right and a man to my left gasping over an ancient tome about some ancient war. I could not believe this bookshop now belonged to me.

Edison returned to the room carrying a china tray on which were two Royal Doulton Rose

Pattern teacups. I recognised the pattern as my mother used to collect antique china.

"Drink up," Edison replied. "I'd stay for a chat, but I'm in the middle of cleaning."

I looked at the cobwebs in the corner of the rooms, the dust that coated the windows. "It could use a little scrub, I guess," I muttered, though I adored the lived-in feel of the shop. "I'm glad the bookshop is in such safe hands. How long have you worked here?"

"Longer than I care to remember. Would you like a tour?"

"Maybe after my cup of tea," I said. I wanted to enjoy my first experience of the bookshop. This, not Rufus's attitude, was the Wild Lime Mountain of my dreams.

"He's awful to everyone," Edison replied, as if he could read my mind.

"Does he always park in the spot I took?" I wanted to rationalise Rufus's behaviour.

"Never," Edison replied. "Drink your tea. You will feel much better soon."

Another voice said, "Tea is always soothing." I looked around, but nobody was there.

CHAPTER 2

It was stereotypical. But that didn't mean it was any easier to bear. My husband had left me for a younger woman. There seemed to be a rash of it in Australia at the moment—in a short space of time, five celebrity football coaches had all left their wives for younger women.

I had fallen out of love with my husband some years ago, but I had been comfortable with my life. Still, I was the one who had to change the lightbulbs and hang paintings on the wall and do all the necessary little handyman jobs around the house.

I guess if I hadn't had the opportunity, I would be still sitting in my old house in Port

Macquarie, nursing my wounds. I pulled the electric hand fan out of my handbag and held it in front of my face until the hot flash passed.

Edison returned and sat opposite me. "I see you have met JenniFur."

"Jennifer?"

"Jenni*Fur*."

I smiled at the pun, but my smile fled at his next words. "JenniFur is your new cat."

"Cat?" I said, rather too loudly. "I thought I was just buying a bookstore." I gestured widely around the room. "The building, the business, the apartment."

Edison appeared taken aback. "You don't like cats?"

JenniFur narrowed her eyes at me. I had always been told that cats narrowed their eyes when they were happy, but she certainly didn't look happy. Surely my imagination was running away with me. "I love cats," I said. "It was just a shock, that's all."

JenniFur jumped into my lap and purred loudly. She kneaded my legs with both front paws. Unfortunately, her claws were not retracted. I bit back a grimace.

"I'm sure you two will get along just fine,"

Edison said. "I must warn you, JenniFur understands every word you say."

I chuckled but stopped when I took another look at his face. He didn't appear to be joking. He was clearly quite eccentric, but what harm could he do? The terms of the bookstore sale were that he continued to work there. Since he had worked in the bookshop for years, according to the contract notes, I doubted his eccentricity had turned away any business. Maybe his eccentricity was even a tourist attraction.

"I'll show you to your room. I've stocked the fridge for you..."

I interrupted him. "That's so kind of you!"

"Not at all, not at all. And JenniFur is very particular about what she eats. I've stuck her routine on the fridge door."

JenniFur stopped sticking her claws in my legs and turned around to fix me with a steely gaze.

I rubbed my eyes. This was all too much. Maybe I was losing my mind. I had heard that people went a little batty at menopause, but I thought it was that sexism. I had never given any credence to it.

Edison was still talking. "Yes, I named her

JenniFur after Jennifer, a friend of mine. Her husband was murdered."

"Murdered?" I repeated. "You're kidding! What, he was murdered right here in Wild Lime Mountain?"

Edison nodded. "Yes, by his long-term mistress, Agatha Jones." JenniFur arched her back and hissed. Edison pushed on. "Agatha confessed to murdering James, and Jennifer hasn't been seen since."

My hand flew to my throat. "You don't think he actually murdered her?"

Edison shook his head. "No, Jennifer is fine. This is top secret, mind you. She has the most horrible and ungrateful children, and they must never know. They think she's in the Caribbean sipping cocktails."

"Where is she?"

He tapped the side of his nose with his index finger. "I'm not at liberty to divulge that information, but I can tell you that Jennifer is quite safe and closer than the Caribbean."

I stopped stroking the cat. "I see. You named the cat JenniFur after her."

Edison chuckled. "You could say that. Come. I'll give you a guided tour. Tomorrow is Monday, and most shops in town are shut on Mondays. You see, the weekend is the busiest tourist time, so most business owners have their weekends on Mondays and Tuesdays here. You don't have to open the shop tomorrow if you don't want to, and it will give you a chance to settle in. I'll stop by in the morning and see if everything is okay."

I thanked him.

"I'll show you to the apartment upstairs now."

I followed Edison up the stairs. The stairs were narrow and wood—maybe old tallowwood—with no carpet on top. I made a mental note not to slip down them if I mopped them. They were awfully steep.

Edison spun around, one finger in the air. "I should have said, but I suppose you would figure it out for yourself soon enough, that the only living room is downstairs. Upstairs are two bedrooms and one bathroom."

I nodded. "Yes, that was on the floor plan."

He nodded vigorously. "Of course, of course."

I expected the bathroom to be hideously original and in desperate need of repair, or maybe it had been renovated in the 1980s and had those hideous orange tiles. I gasped when he flung open the door. It was modern with a gorgeous clawfoot bath in one corner. "It's lovely," I gushed.

"Didn't you see it in the photos?"

I rubbed my eyes. "I don't know. I've had so much happening lately. For some reason, I thought the bathroom was much older."

Edison nodded. "And this will be your bedroom. It's the biggest."

The bedroom looked as though it was straight out of an episode of *Charmed* or maybe from the house in my favourite movie, *Practical Magic*. It was huge with lovely high ceilings.

"I've burnt sage in here," he said, staring at me.

"Sage?"

"White sage. For cleansing spaces."

"I see." I didn't really see, but I followed him to the next bedroom, which was less grand but also big. "The bedrooms are much bigger than they looked in the photos," I said. "It's a veritable Tardis up here." I stared at Edison again. He strongly resembled the first Doctor Who.

Cardboard boxes of my books filled the room. I loved books. I had always escaped into books from the time I was a young child and my teacher read Peter Pan to the class. Books transported the reader to another realm. I couldn't believe my luck, owning a bookstore.

After Edison left, I explored the bookstore more thoroughly. I was in heaven, surrounded by books. It was a dream come true. I found a narrow corridor and in it, to my right, was an old oak door. I tried the brass handle, but it wouldn't budge. I made a mental note to ask Edison.

I returned to the kitchen and looked in the fridge. There was a bottle of wine in there. I reached for it gleefully, but then saw it was red wine, and red wine always made my hot flashes worse. Still, it would be worth it. I shrugged and grabbed the bottle. I didn't feel like rustling up any food. I was far too tired after the seven-hour drive from Port Macquarie through all the Gold Coast traffic and subsequently, all the roadworks up the mountain.

To my delight, the freezer displayed five microwaveable dinners. What's more, there was some ice cream. Maybe Wild Lime Mountain would work out, after all. I sat at the little kitchen table and poured myself a glass of wine. My moment of peace was short-lived, as JenniFur meowed loudly. "Are you hungry?" I asked her.

There was no mistaking the glare. I jumped

up and looked at the list attached to the fridge with a magnet. The list was long, each line starting with, 'JenniFur likes.' It concluded, *JenniFur likes a small snack late at night.*

I fed JenniFur. I dragged myself up the stairs, had a very quick shower—thankfully the water pressure was good, and the water was hot—rummaged through my suitcase, threw on my bathrobe, and flung myself into bed. I imagined I would sleep well after my long day, and as soon as my head touched the pillow, I fell into a deep sleep.

I was awoken with a start. JenniFur was sitting on my chest.

"Hurry!"

I was certain the voice had come from the cat, but that was impossible. She waved a paw at me, and I heard the words, "There's a dead body downstairs."

CHAPTER 3

I sat bolt upright. The cat ran out of the room. I rubbed my eyes. "That's the weirdest dream I've ever had," I said aloud. "It seemed so real."

I turned on the bedside light. A pang of anxiety hit me, and suddenly, I was wide awake. Had there been a noise downstairs, and I had dreamt the cat was telling me something was amiss?

I climbed out of bed and wrapped my fluffy white bathrobe tightly around me. I looked for something I could use as a weapon. There was a brass music stand in the corner of the room. I picked it up, but it was too heavy. Instead, I grabbed my phone and my car keys. I figured I could use my keys as knuckledusters. I sneaked down the stairs, but each one made a loud creaking sound, no matter how hard I tried to be silent.

When I reached the bottom of the stairs, the cat stuck her head around the door leading to the shop. "In here," I was certain she said.

My hands flew to my head. Was I still dreaming? I pinched myself, but it didn't wake me up. I shut my eyes tightly and willed myself awake, but that didn't help either. Maybe I *was* awake, and I had imagined the cat speaking. I walked towards the cat, thoughts of a break-in now less prominent in my mind. Still, I peeked carefully around the door, just in case.

There, in front of me, illuminated by the moonlight, was a large, indeterminable shape on the floor.

My breath froze in my throat. Waves of disbelief flooded over me. Surely this wasn't a body? A *dead* body?

I looked around the room to see if anybody else was there, before edging forward a little and listening again. Not a sound. I tiptoed over to the shape and looked. It was a body all right, the body of a dead man. Maybe a burglar had broken in and died of a heart attack. I rubbed my temples hard. Or maybe he was still alive?

I bent over him and felt for a pulse. There was none. Something wet covered my fingers. When I pulled my hand away, I saw blood. I gasped.

JenniFur meowed. I looked up at her. She was standing next to a pile of broken ceramic shards. I couldn't quite process what I was seeing. A dead man, blood on his head, a pile of ceramic shards. Surely that meant someone had murdered him? But where was that somebody now? Nearby?

I sprinted for the front door, flung it open, and ran to my car. Once safely inside, I called 000.

"What is the nature of your emergency?" the disembodied voice said. "Police, fire, or ambulance?"

"Not fire, but I need police and ambulance," I said breathlessly. "There's a dead man in my shop. I think he's dead. I couldn't find a pulse, but I'm not a doctor. You'd better hurry because if he *is* alive, I don't think he's very well."

I don't remember the rest of the conversation, but the voice told me to wait for the police.

The police arrived shortly, two uniformed officers. I was still sitting in my car with the doors locked. When I saw them, I jumped out and ran over to them. "I'm the one who called," I said. "My name is Nell Darling. I own the bookstore."

The taller man, who identified himself as Senior Constable Tim Thomson, inclined his head to his partner, who went inside. "Wait right here while we have a look around."

The Senior Constable presently emerged. "Tell me what happened," he said.

"I only arrived in town yesterday," I told him. "I bought this bookstore. In fact, I only arrived in town last night. I awoke and thought there was someone downstairs, but when I looked, I found him like that." I shuddered.

"Did you see or hear anybody else?"

I shook my head. "No, but after I found him, I checked for a pulse. That's when I saw the blood, so I thought the person who did it must be close. That's when I ran to my car and called you."

He nodded. "Do you know the victim?"

"No, I only got here yesterday, like I said. I don't know anybody here. Oh, except Edison Chester, who works in the bookstore," I added.

"And what made you wake up?"

I looked at him blankly. "Made me wake up? Oh, I see. I don't really know, to be honest. I was in a deep sleep, and the cat jumped on me. I don't know if that was what woke me up." I narrowed my eyes and tried to remember. "I was worried there was someone downstairs, so maybe I heard a noise. I was a bit afraid to check, but I didn't know what else to do." I could hardly tell him the cat jumped on me, and I imagined she told me there was a body downstairs. "Is he dead?"

"I'm afraid so, Mrs Darling."

"Ms," I said automatically. "I'm divorced."

The officer scribbled something in his notepad. For the first time, I realised he was writing. "We'll need a statement from you."

"What, now?" I said. "Do you want me to come down to the station now?"

He shook his head. "No, but the detectives will be here in the morning. I'm afraid you'll have to shut your shop."

I planted my palm on my forehead. "Oh yes, of course. How long will it stay shut?"

"Until after forensics processes the scene. The detectives will tell you when you can reopen. But for now, Ms Darling, don't go anywhere near that room."

"I won't. Was he trying to rob the place? Or what about his accomplice?"

"His accomplice?"

"I saw some ceramic shards on the floor, and since there was blood on him, I assumed his accomplice knocked him over the head. What if his accomplice is still inside?" My voice rose to a high pitch.

The other officer walked out of the building. "There's nobody around," he said to the sergeant. To me, he said, "The front door was forced open. Is there anywhere you can stay? Can you stay with some friends tonight?"

"No, I'm not from Queensland. I don't know anybody in the whole state. I only just bought the store and arrived here yesterday afternoon. Do you think I'm in danger?" My hand flew to my throat.

The officers exchanged glances. "I suggest you get a locksmith in the morning when the forensics team leaves," Thomson said.

"But how will I shut the front door until then?"

Thomson shrugged. "Maybe you could push something heavy against it, but make sure you don't actually touch the door itself with your hands because we need to take prints. That will happen first thing in the morning. What's your mobile phone number?"

I supplied it and then said, "And would you like the shop number too?"

He said he would, so I flipped open the contacts in my phone and supplied him with that as well.

"You'll be safe for the night," said a voice.

I looked around to see who had spoken, but nobody was there. My eyes fell on JenniFur. Was I completely losing my mind? I was certain the cat was speaking to me. I looked at the officers, and they clearly hadn't heard anything. Maybe it was the shock. Maybe I just needed a good night's sleep. Or maybe it was menopause. I had heard that some women did go a little strange at that time. Yes, having mental issues was surely a symptom of menopause. I didn't know whether to be relieved or alarmed.

The detective handed me his card. "Call us if you hear anything else. We'll drive back past here a couple of times in the night, but call us if you hear anything. Even if you're simply worried and not certain you've heard anything, call us anyway."

I thanked him and assured him that I would.

"You didn't touch anything, did you?" the other officer asked me.

I shook my head. "Oh, I did touch the man to see if he had a pulse before I ran outside and called 000," I said. "My hand felt wet, so that's when I saw the blood, and that's when I figured there was someone else. I was terrified, so I ran to my car to call you."

Senior Constable Thomson nodded. "All right then, you go inside and get something to wedge against the door, maybe a chair would do the trick. The detectives will be here early in the morning and so will forensics. Remember, you will need to keep the shop shut until the detectives give you the clearance. Meanwhile, stay out of that room. There's another entrance, isn't there?"

I nodded. "I have a private entrance."

The other cop spoke up. "I doubt the perpetrator will come back after seeing us here. They're probably as far away as possible now, but do call us if you're concerned."

Once more, I thanked them.

I hurried through the open door and looked around for a chair. I saw a Victorian mahogany balloon back chair upholstered in bright cherry velvet—it was probably a reproduction—and picked it up. It wedged nicely under the door handle. I was glad no windows had been broken in the burglary. I hurried up the stairs with the cat following close behind me.

"You get a good night's sleep, and I'll stand guard," the cat said.

I really was going bonkers! I threw myself into the bed, bathrobe and all, and pulled a pillow over my head so I couldn't imagine anything else.

I was certain I wouldn't be able to catch a wink of sleep, but when I awoke, I was surprised to see it was light outside. I felt groggy and disoriented so hurried into the shower. The hot water was somewhat refreshing.

I walked down the steep stairs and was relieved to see the chair was still wedged under the door handle. A nice coffee machine sat in the kitchen. I hadn't noticed it before. I filled the water compartment and turned it on.

The cat strolled in. I stared at her but thankfully didn't imagine she was speaking. I breathed a long sigh of relief. It was clearly the stress of the previous night that had set my mind off into all sorts of wild imaginations. My relief was short lived, as I heard the words, "I know you were scared after last night, so I brought you a gift."

I stared at the cat. "What—did—you—say?"

The cat waved one paw at me. "I know you were scared after last night, so I brought you a gift to cheer you up."

I clutched my head. I really *had* lost my mind. I was certain I was going to end up in an institution. Or maybe I could go into therapy and somebody could fix me. I would have to make an appointment as soon as possible.

"You haven't seen the gift yet," the cat continued. "It's on your bedroom floor."

Did I go up to my bedroom or not? If I did, it would prove to myself that I thought there *was* a chance the cat was speaking. I forced myself to focus on the coffee pod selection: chocolate, vanilla, caramel, as well as varying intensities of plain coffee.

"The gift!" the cat yelled.

I rubbed my temples hard and sprinted up the stairs as fast as my oncoming arthritis (or maybe the stiffness was simply from a lack of exercise) would allow me.

I walked in the bedroom door and let out a bloodcurdling scream. There, on the floor, was a giant, dead rat. "A rat!" I shrieked.

"You're welcome," the cat said in a smug, self-satisfied tone. She proceeded to purr loudly.

I stepped around the rat and opened the bedroom window. I stuck my head out the window and spotted a garbage can outside. I ran downstairs, out of the private entrance door and grabbed the garbage can. I took off the lid and pulled the can over to the window. I hurried back inside the house and rifled through the kitchen drawers for gloves. There were none, so I picked up a plastic bag. With a plastic bag-covered hand, I picked up the rat by the tail and with a shudder, I flung it out the window.

A nanosecond later, a yell startled me. I looked out the window to see a tall man standing there. His face was bright red. Perched on top of his head was the dead rat.

"I'm Detective Caspian Cole," he said sternly. "Why did you throw a dead rat at me?"

CHAPTER 4

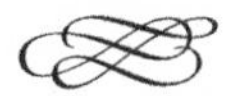

I hurried back downstairs, now out of breath, and flung open the door to the apartment. The detective was standing there, thankfully minus the rat. He stepped aside, and I saw another man behind him. "I'm Detective Cole," he said again, "and this is Detective Sam Stevens. May we come in?"

I nodded and stood aside. "Sorry about that," I said. "My cat caught a rat, and I threw it out the window."

"I noticed." The detective narrowed his eyes. "And I assume you are Mrs Darling?"

"Ms," I said. "I'm divorced. You can call me Nell."

"Do you mind if Detective Stevens has a look around the place?"

I gestured expansively. "Please feel free."

Detective Cole pulled a notepad from his pocket. "I realise you have told the uniformed officers your version of events, but would you please go over what happened last night."

I was flustered. I was still tired from the long drive the previous day as well as from a lack of sleep and from the shock of finding a dead body, a murder victim at that. My words gushed out one after the other. "I went to sleep, and the cat woke me up and said there was a dead body downstairs." I shoved my hand over my mouth when I realised what I had said.

The detective quirked one eyebrow. I realised he was quite attractive, tall with broad shoulders, and I figured around my age. His eyes were an unusual shade of ice blue. He smelt faintly of masculine aftershave, cedarwood and lime. "Did you say the cat spoke to you?"

"No!" I lied. "I meant I had a *dream* that the cat woke me up and said there was a dead body downstairs. Obviously, the cat jumping on me woke me up."

"Go on."

"After the bad dream, I thought I should go downstairs and see if there was anybody there."

"Because the cat told you there was?"

"Yes. I mean, no!"

"So why did you go downstairs?"

"Because I'd had a bad dream, and I was scared." The detective narrowed his eyes. I pushed on. "And then, in the moonlight, I saw the body."

"You didn't turn on a light?"

I took a long deep breath and let it out slowly. "No, because I thought there might be an intruder."

"And why did you think there might be an intruder?"

I was entirely frustrated. Was the man trying to be irritating? Or did he think I was the murderer and was trying to catch me out? I rubbed my left hand over my forehead. "I wasn't sure there was an intruder, but I had woken up with a start, and I wondered whether there could be somebody downstairs. I crept down there just to be on the safe side because I was scared, and that's when I saw the body."

"Go on."

"I hurried over to him and checked his pulse

to see if he was alive."

"And was he?"

"I didn't think so, but I'm not a doctor. Anyway, when I took my hand away, I saw there was blood, and then I saw some pottery shards on the floor. I figured somebody had knocked him over the head. I was scared somebody was still in the house, so I ran outside and locked myself in my car. I called 000."

"Did you have to go back to your apartment first to fetch your phone and your keys?"

I shook my head. "I had the phone with me in case there was an intruder so I could call for help, and I had my car keys to use as a weapon."

He looked surprised, so I demonstrated stabbing someone with my car keys. I stopped when I figured maybe it wasn't such a good idea.

"I see," he said slowly in a manner which suggested he did not. "And did you return to the scene of the crime after calling 000?"

I shook my head vigorously. "No way! Not at all. I certainly didn't do that. I waited until the police officers came. They told me I could go straight back to my apartment after wedging a chair against the shop door. It's still there now unless the other detective has moved it."

"I see," the detective said again. "I'll have a word with Detective Stevens and then come and speak to you again. Would you show me to your kitchen?"

I nodded and beckoned him to follow me. The kitchen was only a short distance away.

"If you will wait here, I'll be back in a moment." He afforded me a curt nod before disappearing through the door. I turned the coffee machine back on. I certainly needed some caffeine. I was halfway through my cup of coffee when the cat came in. I jumped up and put food in her bowl. She purred loudly. I drained the dregs of my coffee cup and wondered how long I would have to wait until the detective returned.

The cat jumped up onto the chair next to me. "That detective thinks you've lost your marbles," the cat said. "He told the other detective you think I speak to you."

I stared at the cat in horror. Could I actually hear her? Surely not! But I hadn't fallen asleep. I was certain I wasn't dreaming.

"You had better shut your mouth, because you look like a goldfish," the cat said.

I continued to stare at the cat. "How can I hear you?"

I looked up to see Detective Cole standing in the doorway. "What did you say?"

"Um, nothing. I was talking to myself because of stress." I was aware my voice was shaky.

"I heard you ask if you could hear somebody."

I thought fast. "Yes, like I said, I was talking to myself. I can't remember where I put my phone."

Thankfully, he did not push it. "How long have you lived here?"

"I arrived yesterday afternoon. I just bought this bookstore."

"Do you have friends, relatives in town?"

"No, I don't know a single soul in the whole of Queensland. In fact, I only met Edison Chester—he's the man who works in the bookstore—when I arrived yesterday afternoon."

"And you haven't met any other locals?"

I shook my head. "No, I arrived late, as I already told you."

Just then, Edison Chester burst into the kitchen. He hurried straight over to me. "Oh, you poor thing. It's all over town that you found a body. Are you all right?"

I did my best not to burst into tears at the show of sympathy. "I'm just tired, that's all," I said. "I had to explain everything to the police last night, and now I've had to repeat everything to the detectives."

Edison looked up at Detective Cole and gasped. He appeared shaken, maybe as he hadn't noticed him at first. It took him a while to speak. "I take it the shop will have to be shut today?"

"Possibly not all day but we will certainly let you know. The forensics team should be here soon. Needless to say, the two of you are to stay out of the area until we give you the all-clear."

Edison nodded. "Sure." To me, he said, "Have you had any breakfast?"

"I've had a cup of coffee."

Edison tut-tutted. "That won't do at all. Would you like some toast, maybe some cereal?"

"Thanks, but I'll get myself some toast." I stood up, but Edison waved me back down. "I'll get it. What will you have on it?"

"Vegemite and peanut butter please."

Edison's eyes widened. "What, on the same piece of toast?"

"Yes, please."

The other detective stuck his head around the door and beckoned to Detective Cole. He whispered something in his ear. Detective Cole walked back over to me and shot me a long, hard look. "You said you haven't met anyone in Wild Lime Mountain apart from this gentleman here?"

I nodded. "That's right."

He stuck a phone in front of me, rather too close to my face. "Can you identify this man?"

"Oh, that's the man who was rude to me yesterday!" I exclaimed.

Edison hurried over to look at the photo. "That's Rufus Rutherford. Was he the victim?"

Detective Cole scowled at me. "Yet you stated you had not met anyone else in town."

"I forgot about him," I protested. "And I didn't exactly meet him. He just yelled at me and said I'd taken his parking spot. It was hardly a meeting."

The detective shot me a look of disbelief. "Ms Darling, I'm afraid you're going to come to the station to make a full statement."

I jumped to my feet, startling JenniFur who hissed at the detective and ran out of the room. "Am I a suspect?"

"We want you to come to the station to help us with our enquiries," Detective Cole said in a monotone.

CHAPTER 5

"I don't know where the police station is. And when do you want me to go there?"

The detective shot me a cold look. "Now."

"Now?" I repeated.

"Did you have somewhere else to be? Your bookstore is shut today, or at least will be until forensics has finished with it."

Edison walked over and tapped my arm. I found his touch reassuring. "I'll mind the shop. I'll open it after the police have finished with it. And don't forget, the bookshop is often shut on Mondays and Tuesdays."

A cold sweat broke out on my forehead. I

turned back to the detective. "But, but how long will it take?" I stammered.

"I can't give you an exact time, but you can follow us. That is, unless you'd rather come in the car with us?"

I couldn't think of anything worse than being escorted away in a police car. "That's okay, I'll follow you."

The detective inclined his head in a perfunctory nod. "Get your things, Ms Darling. We're leaving now."

"My things? You're not going to arrest me?"

Edison patted my shoulder again. "I think he means your handbag."

The detectives walked out of the kitchen. I hurried to fetch my handbag. By the time I got to the road, the detectives had parked in front of my car.

Detective Stevens gave a little wave, and I waved back. I was acutely aware that onlookers were watching. I was sure it would soon be all over town that the new bookstore owner was suspected of murder. Talk about out of the frying pan into the fire! I had thought moving to Wild Lime Mountain would be the start of my new life, the start of my happy and peaceful new life, but things were going from bad to worse.

The drive down the mountain seemed longer than I had remembered from the previous day. My hands were clammy, and a light sweat covered me, despite the fact I had the air conditioning switched on.

At the bottom of the mountain, the detectives turned left at traffic lights, and I continued to follow them. All the while, I was growing increasingly anxious. Surely, they didn't really suspect me?

When we arrived at the police station, an unassuming brick construction which could have been any other building, the detectives turned into a parking area. I didn't know if I was meant to follow them or park out on the main road, but I followed them in.

I got out of the car, half expecting Detective Cole to tell me I had taken somebody's reserved parking spot. Instead, he said, "Follow us."

Detective Stevens swiped a card and then opened a heavy blue door with a glass panel in the top. I followed them inside to a narrow corridor that smelt horribly of pine disinfectant and stale coffee. A low hum reverberated through the building—I assumed it was from ancient air conditioning.

I expected they would show me into a room to be questioned, so I was surprised when I emerged into a small waiting room. I cast a look around the room. It was mostly empty with mismatched and quite uncomfortable looking orange chairs interspersed with dark blue chairs. A tall, thin man was hunched over in the corner wringing his hands, and at the end of the row sat two women happily chatting away.

"Wait here until I see if there's an interview room spare at the moment," Detective Cole barked at me.

"Sure." I sat at the end of the other row, as far away from the other people as I could. My stomach rumbled, and I realised I hadn't had that Vegemite and peanut butter toast. Still, that was the least of my worries.

I too was wringing my hands when Detective Stevens stuck his head around the door. "Ms Darling, would you come with me." It was an order, not a question.

I followed him back into the same corridor, and he stopped at the third door to the left. He held the door open and gestured me inside.

I walked inside and sat on a blue plastic and iron chair, the same style as the ones in the waiting room. I idly wondered if the police department had bought them on sale in a bulk deal.

After I sat down, I glanced up, but Detective Stevens had vanished. I looked around the room. It was a faded shade of beige, and there was a mirror on one wall. Maybe it was a two-way mirror like in the movies. I wondered if they were leaving me here to unnerve me. Well, I was certainly unnerved, and I didn't think I could become even more so. It seemed like a long time before anybody came into the room, but maybe it was only a few moments.

Detective Cole walked in, followed by Detective Stevens. They were each carrying a clipboard and pen. "Would you like a glass of water?" Cole asked me.

I was about to ask if I could have coffee instead when I remembered the lingering aroma of stale coffee that permeated the walls. "No, thank you."

Detective Stevens nodded to a recording device. "Do you have any objection if we record this?"

I shook my head. "No, feel free."

"Would you state your full name, age, and address for the record?"

I did as he asked, but I had barely finished speaking when he announced the time, his name, and Detective Stevens' name.

I noticed a video camera over by the wall, but it wasn't switched on, not as far as I could tell. I wondered if he would ask me if he could video the session.

"Now, tell me in your own words how events unfolded."

I told him about being awoken from a dream—this time I carefully avoided mentioning that I imagined the cat was speaking to me—but he held up one hand, palm outwards, and cut me off. "No, Ms Darling. Please tell me what happened when you arrived in Wild Lime Mountain yesterday."

I told him how I had parked and how Rufus Rutherford had yelled at me for taking his spot.

Detective Stevens leant forward. "And how well did you know the victim?"

"Know him? I didn't know him at all."

"Yet you just said that he accused you of taking his parking spot."

My head was spinning. "Yes, but that doesn't mean I knew him. I only had a brief exchange with him. I had never seen him before, and I didn't see him after that brief exchange either," I added for good measure.

"Until you saw him this morning," Detective Stevens said.

I rubbed my forehead. I was afraid to speak. It seemed everything I said was being turned against me. I nodded.

"Aloud, for the record," Stevens said.

"Yes, that's right." I realised I was raising my voice, but I didn't care. I had done nothing wrong, but I was sure there were plenty of innocent people locked up in prisons. The hair on the back of my neck stood up.

I spent the next ten minutes going through the events of the middle of the night in excruciating detail. When I finished, the detectives made me repeat it several times. I think they were trying to catch me out, to see if my story would change.

"So then, what awoke you?" Detective Stevens asked for the umpteenth time. I was certain I had already answered that in depth at least five times.

The trouble was, I couldn't remember what I had said. "The cat jumped on me and awoke me from my dream. Or maybe a noise downstairs awoke me from my dream, and the cat jumping on me was a coincidence." I glared at them both.

"Didn't you tell me earlier that the cat spoke to you?" Detective Cole asked.

I could see Stevens was doing his best to keep the smirk off his face. "Yes, I did say that, and I assumed I was dreaming," I said. "I *was* dreaming, and something awoke me from my dream."

"The cat, or maybe a noise?" Stevens asked.

"That's right."

"Which one was it?" he pressed me.

I shrugged. "I have no idea."

"Well, Ms Darling, you don't have a criminal record." Cole announced it as though it would be news to me.

"I know that!" I snapped. "And I didn't murder that man. I've just arrived in town. If I was going to murder anybody, it would have been my ex-husband, but he is still very much alive." I regretted the words as soon as they were out of my mouth. The detectives exchanged glances. I doubted either had a sense of humour.

Cole stood abruptly, startling me. "That will be all for now, Ms Darling. Detective Stevens will escort you to have your fingerprints taken, and then you're free to go. Make sure you make yourself available for questioning at a later date. I'm certain we will need to speak with you further so you can help us with our investigation."

"Fingerprinting?" I squealed. "I'm not a criminal! You said so yourself."

Little crinkles formed around the edges of Cole's vivid blue eyes. Maybe he did have a sense of humour, after all. "We need your fingerprints to exclude your prints from those of any intruders," he said. "We have also arranged for Edison Chester to be fingerprinted as well."

"I see," I said with relief.

I too stood up. I had only taken a half step when a uniformed officer stuck her head around the door. Both detectives went into the corridor to speak with her, leaving me standing awkwardly by the chair.

After a short interval, Detective Stevens walked back over to address me. "There were no fingerprints on the murder weapon," he said in an accusatory tone. "The perpetrator wiped them off."

CHAPTER 6

I got into my car and drove away from the police station, shaken. I didn't even take the time to turn on my GPS, something I soon regretted. I had thought I would be able to retrace the route the police had taken, but I was soon lost. There were too many roundabouts, and most of the houses looked alike.

After driving around in circles for some time, I finally gave up. I pulled over on a quieter road and selected my address on the GPS. That calmed my nerves somewhat, but I was shaken to be considered a murder suspect. What's more, Detective Stevens clearly found it suspicious that the murderer had wiped the fingerprints off the murder weapon. Surely, any self-respecting murderer would wipe the fingerprints off a murder weapon? I don't know why that made him suspicious of *me*.

It certainly wasn't a good introduction to my new life in Queensland. And maybe I needed to take more probiotics. I had read recently that gut issues could be linked to depression. I didn't think I was depressed, but I was certainly having problems, because I could swear that cat was speaking to me. I didn't imagine I heard anything else speak to me—no monsters or ghosts, ghouls or goblins.

I shook my head and then stopped at the traffic lights at the bottom of the mountain. No, I needed to see a doctor. Maybe hearing imaginary voices was simply a symptom of menopause.

Once more I fell foul of the roadworks halfway up the mountain. I was at the back of the line, so I switched off the engine and pulled out my phone. I googled symptoms of menopause. They were numerous—hot flashes, mood swings, sleep problems, night sweats, chills, slowed metabolism, weight gain, headaches, joint pain, digestive problems, to name a few—but I couldn't find any mention of hearing imaginary voices.

I had tried five different websites by the time

the traffic had started again, and the last website had, in fact, mentioned mental issues. That gave me hope. Imagining hearing a cat speak was surely a mental issue, and if that could be put down to menopause, all well and good. I mean, menopause would end eventually, right? I know it seemed like it would go on forever, but all things do come to an end. Maybe when menopause had finally gone, I wouldn't hear imaginary cat voices anymore. I certainly hoped so.

Edison had shown me the two parking spots that came with the building. Nevertheless, I cast an anxious look around for somebody wishing to berate me. A nanosecond later, I realised that Rufus wouldn't be able to do that anymore.

I pulled out my keys to unlock the door to my apartment, but Edison appeared. "The police have almost finished, and they said you'll be able to open the shop today," he said by way of greeting, "but I suggest we don't open until tomorrow."

"You don't need to convince me!" I said. I hurried inside and threw myself down on a green velvet armchair in front of the fire, which was not on given it was the middle of summer.

"I'll make you a nice hot cup of tea." Edison

spoke in soothing tones. "Would you like liquorice tea this time? Or chamomile? It's lovely and soothing."

"Coffee, please. I'd love a coffee." I shut my eyes and opened them when the cat jumped into my lap. "Please don't speak to me," I said to the cat. "I'll have to have myself committed."

Thankfully, the cat simply shot me a strange look.

Edison walked in and handed me a polystyrene cup.

"Thank you, but did you buy this?" I said, surprised. "I thought you were going to make me one in the kitchen. I didn't want to put you to any trouble."

Edison sat down opposite me in a large fake leather Chesterfield. It squeaked horribly as he did so, like fingernails on a blackboard. I cringed.

Edison sipped his coffee before answering. "No, that's all right. There's a café next to the bookstore. I let the café owner borrow books, and she gives me free coffees."

I opened my mouth to say something, but he added, "She will give you free coffee too. She prefers physical books to ebooks, so I let her borrow whatever books she likes. I hope you'll continue to do the same as the last owners."

"It sounds like a good deal to me." I certainly liked my coffee, and this was actually the best coffee I had ever had. I said as much.

Edison readily agreed. "Prudence used to be a famous medium."

I waited for him to go on, but when he didn't, I just had to ask. "A medium what?"

Edison clutched his stomach and bent over, laughing so hard I wondered if he would do himself an injury. Finally, he found his voice. "A clairvoyant medium."

"Oh." I felt foolish.

He pushed on. "You would have seen her on TV most likely. Prudence Wallflower?"

"The name is certainly familiar, but I don't go in for that sort of thing. And you say she owns the café?"

"Yes. She married a detective." He must have seen the look of fear flitter across my face, as he hastily added, "A retired detective. He had to leave work on medical grounds, so the two of them moved to the mountain to start a new life."

I could understand that. "That's why I moved here, to start a new life too."

Edison nodded slowly. "What happened at the police station?"

I wiped my hand over my eyes and then remembered with relief I hadn't worn mascara that morning. "It was absolutely ghastly," I admitted. "I'm certain the police think I did it."

Edison shook his head. "Surely not, surely not." He jumped to his feet, lit a tea light candle perched on the mantelpiece, and then picked up a small stick and held it over the candle. A tall flame burst from the little piece of wood. After a moment, he waved it through the air and then approached me.

I shrunk back in fear. "What are you doing?" I squealed.

Edison appeared taken aback. "Haven't you ever been smudged?"

I thought about it. "No, but I have seen it on TV. Don't people use sage? That doesn't look like sage."

"Many people use white sage," he said, "but I prefer Palo Santo sticks. There's a little shop down the road that imports them directly from Peru, and they're the best Palo Santo sticks I've ever come across. These ones are grown sustainably too. This will cleanse you thoroughly. Stand up and stick out your arms so I can get the smoke all over you."

I figured I should humour him. I stood up and held out my arms to the sides, and he wasted no time waving the smoking stick around me. "Sit down and take off your shoes, because it is very important to address the soles of your feet."

I thought that was rather strange, but I wasn't about to say so. I sat down and took off my shoes.

After waving the smoking stick under my feet, Edison placed the remains of the stick in a little metal dish on the mantelpiece before turning to me. "Now, don't you feel better?"

"I suppose so." I did feel a little better, but I figured it was the power of suggestion. Still, I hadn't imagined I had heard the cat speak since I had returned from the police, so maybe things were looking up after all.

The next words dashed my hopes. "I am hungry," said the cat.

I jumped and let out a little shriek.

Edison stared at me. "Are you all right?"

"Did you hear that?"

"Hear what?"

"I'm hungry. Feed me. How can you resist this delightful ball of ginger fluff? Edison always feeds me. You're in charge, so you need to feed me. Now!"

"Edison, the cat is hungry."

He scratched his head. "How did you know that?"

I didn't know how to respond, so I put my shoes back on and hurried to the kitchen. I fetched the cat's food and poured it into a bowl. The cat purred loudly. I turned back to Edison. "Is there a doctor in town?"

He narrowed his eyes. "Are you not feeling well?"

"I need a therapist. Or maybe I need a doctor. Is there a doctor who is also a therapist?"

Edison appeared perturbed. "Well, you *have* had a terrible shock." He stroked his beard. "There's a medical centre at the north of Wild Lime Mountain in the other shopping area."

This was news to me. "There's another shopping area?"

He nodded vigorously. "Oh yes. This street is only for the touros."

"What are touros?"

"Touros—tourists. All the locals do their normal, everyday shopping at the shops on the north side of Wild Lime Mountain. There's a medical centre there as well."

"I'll go there now and see if they can fit me in."

"Thanks for the food," the cat called after me. "Ask Edison to train you how to look after me."

I clutched my throat and hurried back to my car. Once safely in my car and away from the chance of hearing any cats speak to me, I searched the map app on my phone. I readily found the Medical Centre and headed straight there.

It was only five to ten minutes away along a winding mountain road. I was able to park directly at the front of the centre which I took to be a good sign. Clearly, they were not busy.

There was a large tabby and white cat sitting outside. I cast a look around me before directly addressing the cat. "Hello, can you understand what I say?"

The cat just looked at me.

"Can you say something to me? Please! It's important."

The cat yawned and walked away.

I hurried in the front door. A smiling receptionist looked up at me. "I'm new to town," I blurted out. "I only arrived here yesterday. Do you have any free appointments now? I need to see a doctor right away."

The woman continued to smile. "Dr Smith has a free appointment next. She will be able to see you when she's finished with her current patient."

I clutched my stomach with relief. The woman handed me a few sheets of paper and a blue pen. "Please fill out your details along with your medical history."

I walked over to the wall. Nobody else was there. I figured everyone in town must be healthy. I wrote down my name, address, hesitated at my age, but filled it in truthfully anyway, and then answered 'No' to a whole bunch of questions. As I headed back to the receptionist, a man walked out of one of the rooms. The receptionist made another appointment for him and then ducked into the room. She was only gone for a few seconds when she reappeared and said to me, "You can go in now."

Dr Smith appeared to be around fifty. I wasn't good at guessing anybody's age. Her face was smooth and unlined, but her manner was older.

She gestured to a chair sitting opposite her. "So, you're new to town?"

"Yes, I bought the bookstore in Lamington Lane."

She gasped. "Where there was a murder last night?"

"Yes, I found the body," I said. "I am extremely stressed. I'm going through menopause; I've just been through a divorce; I've just moved from New South Wales to Queensland. I bought the bookshop, but I've never owned a business before. My husband said I had no business sense and that I was hopeless with money. And I think I'm going mad, Dr Smith." I said all that without drawing a breath, and then I burst into tears.

"Please, call me Sue." She shoved a box of tissues across the desk to me. "Any one of those life changes would be very hard on a person, and you have had several at once. And you found the body?"

I blew my nose and then said, "Yes. I don't know how I can cope."

"It *is* a lot for one person to take," she said in calming tones. "Moving to a new house is a stressful life event, as is getting a divorce. Starting a business is likewise a stressful life event, and you have also found a murder victim. No wonder you feel you're going mad."

"But that's not why I feel I am going mad," I admitted.

"So, tell me the reason."

Now that I was here, I was horribly embarrassed. "Well, I don't know how to tell you," I said. "It's going to sound extremely strange. I mean, I *know* it sounds extremely strange. I thought it was a symptom of menopause, and when I googled it, it did say that mental problems can be a symptom of menopause. Is that true?"

"Certainly. Do go on."

"This will sound crazy, but I imagine I can hear a cat talking to me."

She did look shocked then. "You think you can hear cats talk?"

I shook my head. "No, no, no. Not cats, only one cat. The cat that came with the bookshop. I know it sounds crazy, and I thought somebody was playing a prank on me, but Edison Chester wouldn't do a thing like that. I mean, I've only known him since yesterday, but he seems too nice to perform such a terribly unkind prank."

"Let's take your blood pressure," she said.

After she did so, she said, "It's only up a little, and that's perfectly understandable with what you've been through. It's certainly nothing to worry about. I'll order a blood test to see if you have something out of balance." She sat back in the chair opposite me. "When did this start?"

"Only when I arrived yesterday," I said. "Actually, it happened in the middle of the night."

"So, it started happening before you found the murder victim?"

I nodded. "Yes, that's right."

The doctor tapped a pen on her chin. It was a sparkling gold pen. It distracted me, and I was going to ask her where she got it—I'd love a pen like that—when she asked, "Did you see the cat's mouth move?"

I thought that an awfully strange question, so much so, that I hesitated a while before answering. "No, actually, the cat's mouth doesn't move at all."

"Do you think you are actually hearing the cat speak or hearing the cat's thoughts?" The blank look on my face must have prompted her to add, "That is, do you think you're psychic, clairaudient? That is to say, a psychic who claims they can hear the thoughts of others?"

I threw up both hands to the ceiling. "I don't have a clue! I haven't ever given any thought to such things, but Edison told me that the lady who works in the café next to the bookstore was a famous medium. A clairvoyant medium," I added for good measure. "Maybe I should speak to her."

The doctor looked alarmed. She tapped the desk. "No, I wasn't for a moment suggesting that you can actually hear the thoughts of the cat. No, not at all. So, you said you're from Port Macquarie?" I nodded. She pushed on. "Were you seeing anybody there?"

"No, I'm not ready for dating. My divorce has only just come through."

The doctor shot me a long, hard look. "I meant, seeing a therapist."

"Oh." I felt foolish. "No, because I haven't imagined I've heard cat voices until now. It only started yesterday," I added for the umpteenth time.

"Well then, you *have* been under a considerable deal of stress. Menopause can indeed cause mental issues. It's likely you need hormone replacement therapy. If the blood test doesn't show up any imbalances, let's leave it for a few more days, and if this persists, I'll have to refer you to someone."

"A therapist?"

She shook her head. "A psychiatrist. It's likely you will need medication."

My hand flew to my throat. "Medication?"

The doctor droned on about going to a pathologist for the blood test and then coming back and seeing her in a few days. I nodded but thought it wouldn't hurt to go to the coffee shop next door to speak with Prudence Wallflower.

Either I had gone crazy, needed hormone replacement therapy, or had suddenly become psychic. Maybe all three.

CHAPTER 7

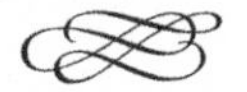

When I got back to the shop, the door was locked, and there was a sign on the door saying we were closed for the day. I walked around to my apartment door, unlocked it, and let myself in. I walked through the adjoining door to the shop. "Are you here, Edison?" I called out.

"In here," said a muffled voice.

I walked in, yet to my dismay, there was no sign of Edison. The fat ginger cat, JenniFur, was sitting on a table on top of a book. "He said he won't be long," the cat said nonchalantly.

I walked over to stare at the cat. Sure enough, her mouth hadn't moved. I don't know what difference it made, but I felt it was worth noting.

"I might need hormone replacement therapy," I said to the cat.

She waved one white-tipped paw at me. "Oh, because you think you are imagining things? Well then, imagine how I feel! I used to be a human, and I turned into a cat."

I gasped. "What, why, when?"

"Somebody was trying to murder me, so I turned myself into a cat," the cat said smugly. "And I like being a cat. People wait on me and give me whatever I want."

I clutched my head and sprinted from the apartment. I wondered if I should call the doctor and ask how long before she could start me on the hormone replacement therapy or give me a referral to a psychiatrist for drugs, lots of drugs, but then I smelt the alluring fragrance of coffee. Prudence Wallflower!

I would ask her. No doubt she would think I was mad, but I just had to know. Maybe she wouldn't think I was mad considering she was a clairvoyant medium.

I walked around the side of my building into the front door of the coffee shop. Luckily for me, there were no customers.

A woman walked out to the counter. "Are you

Prudence?" I asked her. When she nodded, I added, "I'm Nell Darling, the new owner of the bookshop, but you must already know that."

She chuckled and shook her head. "Oh no, not at all. I see Edison has told you I'm a clairvoyant medium. That doesn't mean I'm psychic."

In spite of my panic over the possibility of being stark raving mad and delusional, I was intrigued. "Is there a difference?"

Prudence pursed her lips, and I had the sensation she'd had to explain this many times. "Yes, as a matter of fact. I receive impressions from deceased people. I'm not psychic. I don't have premonitions, and I can't tell what others are thinking and so on. All I do is receive impressions from those who have passed on."

"Like Rufus?"

Prudence frowned. "I haven't received any impressions from him, but I doubt he'd come here to seek me out. Besides, my husband is very much against me investigating."

Now I really *was* intrigued. "Why?"

"Levi himself was nearly murdered—he's a former detective, you see—and I've had a few close calls while investigating murders. We left our old town when Levi retired for medical reasons and we moved here. These days, he's a consultant, and I have the café. Now that there's been a murder, Levi wants us to go on a holiday up to the Whitsundays. We're leaving tomorrow, and my assistant, Daisy, will mind our dog and run the coffee shop for me." She chuckled. "The deal is still on for free coffee for you and Edison."

I bit my lip and thought things over. "That's not why I came. I wanted to ask you a question about being psychic." She frowned and opened her mouth, so I quickly added, "I know you say you're not psychic. It's just that I'm wondering if *I* might be. Can, um, psychic ability develop later in life or are people born with it?"

Prudence shrugged. "I think most people are born with it, but it tends to diminish when they reach an age when they start to rationalise things. Still, it could always come back later. What makes you think you're psychic?"

I looked over my shoulder, but there was still no sign of customers. "It's awfully embarrassing," I told her, "and, in fact, I've just been to the doctor to see if it could be a symptom of menopause."

"A symptom of menopause!" Prudence appeared entirely surprised.

I took a deep breath. "I think I can hear the cat speaking."

Prudence's eyes grew wider. Neither of us spoke. After what seemed an age, Prudence was the one to break the silence. "I take it you don't mean that you know when the cat is hungry and things like that."

I shook my head. "I believe it's called clairaudience. I can actually hear the words aloud. Have you ever heard of that?"

Prudence appeared to be thinking over. "Yes, I've heard of clairaudience. It's very rare, and I've only heard of instances where a person can sometimes hear what other people are thinking or maybe hear messages from spirits. I've never heard of anybody hearing what an animal is thinking. When did this all start?"

"Only yesterday! It only happened after I arrived here yesterday, and I tried speaking to another cat and nothing at all happened. It's only this one particular cat."

"JenniFur?"

"That's right." I thought Prudence must think I was quite strange, to say the least.

"Normally, I would think it is impossible, but there is something different about JenniFur. I can't put my finger on it, but she's not like a normal cat."

I agreed. "I've just been to see one of the local doctors, and she thinks I might need hormone replacement therapy, and if that doesn't work, I might need to see a psychiatrist for drugs."

Prudence narrowed her eyes. "Until late last century in Australia, having a psychic experience was a certifiable act. Somebody could be institutionalised against their will for having a psychic experience."

Now *that* surprised me. "You're kidding!"

Prudence shook her head.

"So, do you think it's at all possible? I mean, do you think there is any possibility I could be hearing a cat's thoughts?"

"It does sound really weird, but I wouldn't dismiss it out of hand," Prudence said slowly. "All my life, I had only ever received impressions from the dead. I was doing a show when I actually saw a ghost with my very own eyes. He looked as solid as you."

I gasped. "You're kidding! You actually saw a ghost with your own eyes?"

Prudence chuckled. "That's where it gets interesting." Before she could say any more, three women walked into the shop. Prudence beckoned her assistant out to serve them and then took me by my arm and led me to the courtyard adjacent to the building. When we were standing under a flowering jacaranda tree, she said, "I thought he was a ghost, but it turns out Levi was in a coma and was somehow appearing to me."

"Levi? Your husband?"

Prudence smiled. "Yes, that's when we met. I know it sounds absolutely impossible, which makes me think you might really be hearing the cat." She hesitated before adding, "At least it's a possibility. And you say it's never happened to you before?"

I shook my head. "No, it's never happened to me. I'm recently divorced. My husband was allergic to cats, so I couldn't have one. I intended to get a cat when I moved here, but as it turned out, JenniFur came with the bookshop."

"You mentioned menopause. I have heard that some people realise they're clairvoyant mediums or psychic for the first time when they're going through menopause," Prudence said.

"Maybe it's called *the change* for all sorts of reasons."

I scratched my head. "Maybe you're right."

"What sort of things does the cat say to you?"

I remembered the cat told me that she used to be a person once, but I was hardly about to tell that to Prudence. Prudence would really think I had lost my marbles if I said that. "She told me that she's hungry; she told me the police would suspect me, and she was the one who told me there was a dead body downstairs. She woke me up last night."

"*Do* the police suspect you?"

I nodded vigorously. "Detective Cole and Detective Stevens made me go to the police station for questioning," I told her. "I definitely got the impression they see me as a serious suspect."

"Did you know the victim before you moved here yesterday?" Prudence asked me.

I shook my head again. "No, I had never met him, but as soon as I arrived in town, he yelled at me that I had taken his parking spot. Lots of people watched him yell at me, and the police know that."

"It's hardly a motive for murder."

I agreed. "Can you think of *anybody* who would want to murder him?"

Prudence frowned. "Plenty of people, I'd say. I mean, plenty of people disliked him. Rufus was a commercial landlord. He owned several of the shops, and he didn't treat his tenants fairly. And there's talk around town that he didn't get on with his neighbours."

"Was he wealthy?" I asked her.

Prudence nodded. "Oh, I see you're thinking of the heir as a suspect. Rufus does have a son who is a golf professional. I think he lives in Hope Island." I must have looked blank, because she added, "It's just over half an hour's drive from here. I don't know if Rufus was wealthy or if he had any other relatives, but I definitely know he has a son."

"I hope the police soon find out who did it. Detective Stevens told me that the fingerprints had been wiped off the murder weapon. He said it to me in an accusatory tone as if he thought I was the murderer."

Prudence raised one eyebrow. "What *was* the murder weapon?"

I shrugged. "I think it was a pottery item. Edison would know. When I found the body, there were broken ceramic pieces lying around him. Somebody must have hit him over the head. I suppose the fact that I had an argument with him the day before and he was murdered in my shop makes me look suspicious in the eyes of the police."

Prudence waved her finger at me. "Please don't take that as motivation for solving the case. I'm sure the detectives are competent and will soon find the murderer."

"I hope you're right."

The two of us walked back into the coffee shop. I thanked Prudence for her help and walked outside of the building. I was dismayed to see Detective Cole and Detective Stevens getting out of a car. When they saw me, they hurried over to me.

Detective Cole shoved a piece of paper under my nose. "We have a warrant to search your place."

I was horrified. "A search warrant? For my apartment or my shop?"

Detective Stevens scowled at me. "Both."

CHAPTER 8

I was relieved when Edison walked out of the shop door. "What's this about?"

Detective Cole showed him the warrant.

Edison stood aside and waved them inside.

"Why do they have a warrant to search the place?" I asked him. "I thought they searched the place this morning."

"Maybe they have new information." Edison's brows furrowed.

"What sort of information?"

Edison shrugged. "Let's go inside to make sure they don't make a mess. They always make a mess when they search places on TV."

I hurried after him into the shop, but the detectives had already gone through the door into my apartment. Something occurred to me. "On TV, don't uniformed officers help the detectives search?"

Edison appeared to be at a loss. "I have no idea. Maybe it's good there are only two of them. They won't make as much mess."

Edison seemed concerned about mess, but something was eating away at me. Why did they want to search the place a second time? Did that mean they *really* thought I was the murderer?

I was sick to my stomach. I walked over to the fireplace and sat down in the big Chesterfield. I always found fireplaces comforting, and even though this fire wasn't lit, it did offer me a small measure of comfort. My comfort was short lived when JenniFur appeared and sat on the couch opposite me.

"They're looking for poison," she said. "I overheard them talking. They think I'm just a cat."

"But you *are* a cat," I said and then looked up horrified when Detective Cole strode into the room.

"What did you say?"

"I was talking to the cat," I said.

"You do realise that in Australia you can't get

a reduced sentence on the grounds of diminished responsibility?" He nodded slowly as he spoke.

"I have no idea what you're talking about," I snapped.

JenniFur meowed and then said, "He's saying you can't make a plea on grounds of insanity like they can in some overseas countries."

"I am *not* pleading insanity!" I snapped. "I didn't do it!"

The detective raised his eyebrows and left the room.

I was quite shaken. The detective obviously thought I imagined the cat was speaking to me—but then, I *did* imagine the cat was speaking to me! Still, Prudence did say it was possible that I could hear the cat's thoughts.

The door creaked, and I looked up, fearful it was one of the detectives. To my relief, it was Edison. I decided I might as well tell him. JenniFur moved aside to make room for Edison and then jumped onto his lap, proceeding to knead his legs with her paws. "Ouch," Edison explained, followed by, "Ouch!" To me, he said, "JenniFur doesn't retract her claws."

"Why don't you retract your claws?" I asked the cat. "You know it hurts."

JenniFur purred loudly. "Because I'm a cat, and that is what I do."

I looked up to see Edison regarding me strangely. "There's something I have to tell you," I said, "but before I do, I need you to know that I went to speak with Prudence at the coffee shop, and she thinks I might not be stark raving mad."

Edison drew one hand over his forehead. My heart went out to him. He loved the bookstore. Someone had been murdered in it, and what's more, he had to put up with an entirely new bookstore owner. He wasn't having an easy time either. "Okay Edison, you might think I am crazy, but ever since I got here, I'm certain I can hear JenniFur's thoughts."

I expected Edison to look shocked. "I see. Have you ever heard any other cats' thoughts?" he asked in a monotone.

"No. I can only hear JenniFur's thoughts. That is why I went to the doctor..."

"And what did the doctor say?"

I thought Edison was taking this rather too well. "She said I might need hormone replacement therapy or see a psychiatrist for some sort of medication."

Edison chuckled. "And what does JenniFur say to you?"

I took a deep breath and let it out slowly. "That's what Prudence asked me. JenniFur told me that the police suspect me, and she also told me that she used to be a person and when somebody tried to murder her, she turned into a cat."

Edison smiled and nodded. "Well, I'm glad you can communicate with JenniFur. Yes, she was a lovely lady when she was a human, a friend of mine, Jennifer Smothering. I told you about her before, remember? Anyway, Jennifer's husband, James, cheated on her with a lady by the name of Agatha Jones. Jennifer must have discovered this, because I suspect Agatha tried to murder her too." He chuckled. "Oh yes, you just told me JenniFur said as much."

This was all too much for me. I leant forward, my head in my hands. Oblivious to my distress, Edison continued his tale. "Jennifer in cat form turned up here one night. I thought she was a stray, although she did look familiar. The next morning, somebody told me that Agatha Jones had been arrested by the police. Agatha confessed to the police that she had murdered Jennifer's husband, James, and she said she saw Jennifer turn into a cat. That's when I realised that JenniFur was of the, um, I mean to say, well, I suppose you could say, a *witch*."

Now I really thought I had gone mad. I jumped to my feet. "A witch!" I shrieked. "It was one thing to believe I could hear a cat speak to me, but now you're expecting me to believe in witches, and that a human turned into a cat!"

I sat down and promptly burst into tears.

Edison jumped to his feet, I assumed to console me, but JenniFur said, "Get a grip. You don't see me bursting into tears, and I was the one who turned myself into a cat. You can hear me because we're related."

I stopped crying. "We're related?" To Edison, I said, "I am related to JenniFur?"

Edison passed me a box of tissues. JenniFur arched her back. "We both have red hair."

"Yes, but everyone in the world who has red hair isn't related," I pointed out.

JenniFur hissed. "Of course we're not witches. For somebody who reads a lot of books, Edison gets his words mixed up at times. He simply means women with power. Our bloodline comes into power at the time of menopause. That's when our powers start to show."

The door flew open once more, and Detective Stevens marched straight into the room. "Edison Chester, would you accompany us to the station? You too, Ms Darling."

Detective Cole shook his head. "We've already questioned Ms Darling."

Stevens looked surprised. "But in light of this new evidence…"

Detective Cole interrupted him. "I will question Ms Darling here. You can take Mr Chester for questioning."

A dread chill ran up my spine. The cat said they were looking for poison—had they found it? I dared not ask, but they had certainly found something. I supposed I was about to find out.

Detective Cole sat opposite me in Edison's newly vacated chair. "Do you know if the victim had any friends?"

I shrugged. "Doesn't everybody have friends? I mean, some close, some not so close." I realised I was rambling, so I added, "But I have already told you this! I had never heard of the man in my life or ever seen him before until he yelled at me for taking his parking spot yesterday afternoon, and why would I want to murder somebody just for yelling at me?"

The detective pulled a note pad and a pen from his pocket. "Tell me how the victim looked when you saw him."

"Do you find him attractive?" said the cat.

"Hush!"

Detective Cole leant forward. "Excuse me?"

"I have already specified how he looked in my statement."

The detective's expression was impassive. "Humour me."

"Dead. He looked dead."

"Yet you said you checked for signs of life."

"Yes, because it was the right thing to do, and I'm not a nurse or a doctor. He looked dead to me, but what would I know? That is why I checked for signs of life." I said each word through clenched teeth. "You asked me how he looked, and I told you he looked dead. That's the truth." I knew I was being defensive, but then again, I was quite aware I was a suspect. Probably the prime suspect. Maybe the *only* suspect.

"What do you think woke you? Try to remember, Ms Darling. Anything you can remember could be a help. Can you try to recall what woke you up?"

I shut my eyes tightly, as if that would help me remember. "It was the cat jumping on me." I pointed to JenniFur.

"Do you recall hearing any noises?"

I shook my head. The detective narrowed his eyes. "Somebody hit the victim over the head, and he fell to the ground. Surely, that would have made a noise."

"Yes, I am certain it made a noise," I said, "only I don't recall hearing it."

"I heard it," JenniFur walked over to me, purring loudly. "I heard a loud noise. I went down to check and saw him lying there."

"Did you see anyone else?" I asked her.

The detective shot me a penetrating look. "Excuse me? What did you say?"

I thought fast. "I said that I didn't see anyone else. When I came downstairs, I only saw the victim. The murderer must've been nearby at the time." I shuddered. "Why did you take Edison away for questioning? And what were you looking for with your search warrant?"

"I'm afraid I can't discuss the case with you, Ms Darling."

I suddenly grew hot. I grabbed a magazine on the coffee table next to me and fanned myself furiously. "He wasn't murdered by a knock over the head with the ceramic thing. If he was, you wouldn't have come back."

When he didn't respond, I fanned myself more furiously. I felt as though my insides were on fire. "Look, Detective, I have just been through a terrible divorce. I came to Queensland to live a happy life. I came to what I was told was a nice, peaceful small town in the Gold Coast hinterland. I wasn't the one who yelled at the victim about the parking spot—he yelled at me. I have done nothing wrong, yet I have been dragged down to the police station and questioned, and it's clear that you think I am a murder suspect. I have had the worst twenty-four hours of my life. The fact you have a search warrant after you have already searched the place means new evidence has come to light, and I can only assume that was a result of the autopsy. I am not stupid, I'll have you know, and I watch a lot of cop shows on TV."

I didn't know if I imagined it, but I thought the detective's lips quirked upwards with my last remark.

"I will tell you that there is a possibility the

blow to the head was not, in fact, the cause of murder. I am afraid I can't answer any further questions. Now, Ms Darling, please keep yourself available for questioning. I am sure we will need to speak with you at a later date." He looked at his phone. "I have to make a call. I'll be back soon." With that, he walked away.

I wondered if the police had gained entry to the locked room. They hadn't asked me for a key, which was just as well as I didn't have one. I hurried into the dark corridor. The door had gone. I stared again. I was certain this was the place—but where was the door? In front of me was a wall, and no doorway was in sight. Could I have been mistaken?

"I am hungry."

I swung around and looked at the cat. "Sure. JenniFur, do you know if there was ever a door in this wall?"

"I don't feel like tuna," she said. "I want chicken."

"Okay." I realised I wouldn't get any sense out of her. I crossed to the fridge and pulled out the glass container with the cat food. I dropped some into her bowl. I figured I should eat something, but the fridge didn't have much apart from cat food. I remembered the microwavable dinners in the freezer. To my delight, there was a microwave curry. I didn't even pause to read the directions. I simply took it out of the cardboard packet, peeled the plastic back a little, and stuck it in the microwave.

I was standing there watching the microwave when JenniFur spoke. "They found a bottle of poison in your laundry room," she said.

I spun around. "Why didn't you tell me that before?"

"I was hungry," she said. "Cats can't think properly on an empty stomach." She licked one paw and rubbed it over her ears.

"Don't stop there," I said. "What was the poison?"

"1080."

"1080?"

"You might need to go to the vet to have your ears cleaned out," JenniFur said. "Yes, that is what I said, 1080. It's a poison, you know."

"I've heard of it. I didn't think it was a household poison, not a freely available one."

JenniFur stopped licking her other paw to respond to me. "It isn't. That is why the police are suspicious. And now they are questioning that nice man, Edison. Do you know what this means?"

I didn't. "What does it mean?" I asked her.

"Somebody poisoned the victim and then knocked him over the head. They certainly wanted to make sure he was dead."

"I see."

JenniFur hissed. "You didn't let me finish. That wasn't my point. My point is, somebody poisoned the victim and lured him into your shop. Then they hit him over the head and planted the poison in your laundry room. Somebody is trying to frame you for the murder."

CHAPTER 9

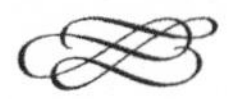

A lightbulb moment. I do have them occasionally. If the victim *was* murdered by 1080 poison, that would prove I was actually hearing JenniFur's thoughts, and I hadn't gone mad.

I hurried upstairs to my bedroom. The detectives hadn't made a mess at all, much to my relief. I grabbed my laptop and opened it. The internet took a while to kick in. I muttered a few rude words about my internet provider and then typed '1080.'

To my surprise, 1080 was banned in all countries with the exception of Australia and New Zealand. I discovered the chemical name was sodium fluoroacetate and that the fatal dose for humans was one-half to two milligrams per kilogram. I was mathematically challenged, but after some mental gymnastics and the help of the calculator on my phone, I figured that one third of a cup would have been more than enough to despatch the victim.

The next site I found said it was colourless, odourless, and that in powder form it looked like flour.

JenniFur jumped onto my bed, sending cat fur flying. "Anything interesting?"

I shrugged. "I can't find any cases of it being used as a murder weapon, although it did say that it would kill a human in thirty minutes to two hours."

"Why did you say that wasn't interesting?"

"I didn't say that!" I shook my head—now I was arguing with a cat. "It's hard to get. Somebody needs a licence to procure it."

JenniFur jumped onto a chest of drawers and knocked a bottle of perfume off the edge. She jumped down and swiped at it with her paw, rolling it under my bed. "It's Australia."

I leant under the bed and snatched up the perfume bottle. "Your point?"

"Banned poisons are everywhere. Go to any

farm, and you'll see what I mean. One barn probably has enough stuff to wipe out a whole town."

I was on edge. There was nothing I could do until Edison returned, so I walked downstairs to explore the bookshop—*my* bookshop. Being under suspicion of murder had quashed all my excitement at moving to a new state and buying the bookstore.

I loved the smell of books. I walked along looking at the new books and then walked down to the back of the store. The light down there was different, mellow somehow, as though it was lit by candles although, of course, I didn't see any candles. I looked at some gold embossed, leather bound volumes—the whole collection of Plato's works, and Plutarch's *Lives*.

I had forgotten the bookshop had a substantial second-hand book collection, and these all looked uncommon, if not rare. Still, they were not in a climate-controlled setting, so I figured they weren't overly valuable.

As I walked around the bookstore, my excitement grew. Once I was cleared of the murder, I could actually enjoy myself here. I let out a happy sigh. I could do as much reading as I wanted. I owned the building and the business outright thanks to the property settlement, so I wouldn't have any terrible financial worries.

I was certain the bookstore would make enough for me to live on. I figured I wouldn't have to work terribly hard, at least not long hours seven days a week, and that would leave me lots of time for reading.

I was broken from my happy thoughts by a knock on the bookshop door. There was a closed sign on the door. Who could it be?

I flung open the door to see Edison standing there. "Why didn't you let yourself in?" I asked, surprised.

"I didn't like to, given it was shut for the day," he said.

I beckoned him inside. "Come on, I'll make you some coffee." I quickly amended that to, "Tea."

I noticed his usually already pale face was white and drawn. He sat down at the kitchen table, and I turned to the collection of glass jars, all variously labelled with types of tea. I tried to think of soothing varieties. "Would you like some chamomile tea? Or maybe lemongrass?" I picked up a glass jar and peered at the label. "This one is a mixture of liquorice root and orange peel, along with some other things."

"Yes, that one will do nicely, thank you." His tone was somewhat absent.

I reached for the coffee pods and then thought the better of it. I would be awake all night if I had coffee at this time of day. Instead, I put enough tea leaves for two in the teapot.

I was impatient to hear what the police had said, but I didn't want to upset Edison. After what I thought was a polite interval, I said in the calmest tone I could muster, "Did the police give you a hard time?"

Edison's eyes flickered from side to side. He stirred his tea, although there was no sugar in it. "It was rather unpleasant."

I waited for him to say more, but when nothing more was forthcoming, I added, "Did they treat you like a suspect?"

He took a sip of tea and placed his cup back in the saucer. "I am afraid they asked questions about you."

My hand flew to my throat. "Me? They still think I did it?"

Edison bit his lip and took another sip of tea.

"What exactly did they say?" I prompted him.

"It seems to be related to whatever they found in the apartment."

"Did they say what it was?" I leant forward eagerly.

He shook his head. My stomach sank. Before I could say anything, the cat jumped up onto one of the seats at the table. "Tell him about the 1080," she said.

"The cat says they found 1080 poison."

I thought Edison would be shocked by my disclosure, but once again, he didn't seem to find my mention of the cat speaking at all strange. That, in itself, was strange. Still, Edison was convinced JenniFur used to be a person. He nodded slowly. "That would make sense."

"Excuse me?" I wondered if I would faint. The room seemed to be spinning slightly. I wondered if I should put my head between my legs but instead took a long, deep breath. "Why would it make sense?"

"The police asked me if I'd had any contact with your husband."

"My husband?" I squealed. "What on earth does he have to do with anything?"

"The police said he works for the New South Wales Office of Environment and Heritage."

I scratched my head. "Yes, in an administrative capacity. What does that have to do with…" My voice trailed away. I tapped myself on the side of the head. "1080! Anybody from the Office of Environment and Heritage should be able to get easy access to it. Do they think my husband and I were in it together?"

Edison appeared entirely confused. "I don't understand a word of what you have said." He drained the rest of his tea.

I wondered how he did so, given it was so hot. I refilled his cup. "JenniFur told me the police had found a bottle of 1080 poison in my laundry room. When you were away, I did some research on it. I found out that it's only legal in Australia and New Zealand, and somebody needs a permit for it. Permits, you see, are issued by the Office of Environment and Heritage as well as several other organisations."

Edison appeared to be thinking it over. "I wondered why they would suspect you when you had just arrived in town. It didn't make sense, because you had barely met the victim. Sure, he did yell at you, but it was clear to all the onlookers that he had never met you before. Nobody would murder someone just for yelling at them in the street, the first time they had met them. No, it makes sense if the police think you and your husband were involved in it together."

"It does?" I squeaked. "But it doesn't make sense to me. My husband and I are divorced, and it was an acrimonious divorce."

JenniFur put her front paws on the table. "That would be a good cover."

"What would?" I asked her.

"Your divorce would be a good cover. This could be how the police see it. Hear me out." She waved one paw in the air. "Your husband has had dealings with the victim—don't ask me what—and wants to do away with him. You both pretend you're in it together. You both go through a divorce and pretend to be at each other's throats as a cover."

JenniFur sat back on her hind legs. "You just happen"—she made air quotes with her front paws—"to move here to a town where the victim lives, and you do away with him. As you have never met him, you are not suspected, and your husband has the perfect alibi. He is in another town at the time and nobody would think you are in it together because you had a nasty divorce."

"But that's preposterous!" I said.

"What did JenniFur say?" Edison asked me.

I repeated everything that she had said, followed by, "But surely the police don't think that."

Unfortunately, Edison agreed with the cat. "That does make sense."

"Well, it doesn't make sense to me." That seemed to be my mantra of the evening. I thought about it some more. "Wouldn't they have to prove my husband knew Rufus?"

"Of course they would have to prove that." Edison shot me a reassuring smile. "Rufus used to live in New South Wales. He only moved here ten years ago."

"Whereabouts did he live before that?"

"I can't remember." Edison scratched his head. "Coffs Harbour, maybe. Yes, I think that's what he said."

My spirits sank. "Coffs Harbour isn't all that far from Port Macquarie, and I think it's within my husband's administrative area. Would the fact that they lived about an hour and a half apart make the detectives suspicious?"

"It would make them suspicious for sure, but it would look rather silly if it ever came to court." Edison leant over and patted my hand. "And I am sure it would never get to court. It seems rather spurious evidence."

"I hope so." I sipped my tea. It had cooled off considerably, so I swallowed it all in one gulp. I wondered how long it would take to soothe my nerves. "Edison, do you really think I can hear JenniFur' speak?"

"Yes, of course."

I stared at him. What if we were both mad? While I was considering this, Edison pushed on. "You know, the 1080 should prove it."

I was at a loss. "Prove what?"

"Prove that you can hear JenniFur. Otherwise, why would the police think your husband was involved? They mentioned your husband to me because whatever they took from your laundry room must be a poison that could be issued by the Office of Environment and Heritage."

"I suppose there are several poisons that are issued by the Office of Environment and Heritage."

Edison narrowed his eyes. "Are you sure?"

I had to admit that I wasn't.

"And 1080 is definitely one of them. Doesn't this prove to you that you can hear JenniFur?"

"Yes, I think so!" My spirits were lifted. I

jumped up and grabbed Edison's hands and danced around the room with him. "I thought I was absolutely bonkers," I said. "Maybe I can hear the cat, after all! I am not mad!"

I could almost hear my husband's words in the background: *Nell, don't make a fool of yourself in public. Nell, keep your hand gestures to a minimum in public. Nell, don't laugh so hard at this movie; you're showing too much emotion.* I laughed even louder. I was free of my husband; I was living in a new town, and I hadn't lost my marbles.

Still, there was the whole matter of a cat talking to me, but Edison didn't seem to think it was strange, and I would just have to get used to it.

My phone rang, and I didn't check the caller ID. I picked it up and answered it automatically. "Hello?"

I was dismayed to hear my husband's voice. "What's going on?" he snapped. "What have you been up to?"

"What do you mean?" I said defensively, and then silently berated myself for feeling the need to be defensive with my ex-husband. I was no longer living under his cloud.

"The police called me and asked me if I knew

some random man. Apparently, he was murdered in your shop. Did you have anything to do with it?"

I said a few rather unladylike words that made the cat gasp, and then I hung up.

CHAPTER 10

Once more, I was awoken in the early hours of the morning. I sat bolt upright. "Don't tell me there's been another murder!"

JenniFur padded over the blankets to me. "No, but something was puzzling me when I was throwing up a furball."

I rubbed my eyes and reached for my phone. "It's only three in the morning!" I protested.

JenniFur appeared unperturbed. "Why was Rufus poisoned *and* hit over the head?"

"I expect they really wanted to make sure he was dead," I said. "Maybe the murderer poisoned him and then hit him over the head in self-defence."

JenniFur meowed loudly and then added,

"Nonsense! You're not very good at this, are you? He was hit over the back of the head, if you hadn't noticed. A blow to the back of the head is hardly a defensive wound."

I had to admit she was right. "Then how do you explain it? Do you have any theories?"

JenniFur licked her right paw before answering. "Maybe he was already dead when he was hit over the back of the head. Maybe he was already dead when he was brought to your shop."

"But what purpose..."

JenniFur interrupted me. "For the purpose of framing you, of course. Isn't it obvious? The murderer must have already planned Rufus's murder before you came to town. That part is obvious too. When they saw you have an argument with Rufus, they must have suddenly decided they would poison him and frame you. You'd make a good scapegoat, because half the town saw him yelling at you."

I was only half listening. I was wondering whether I'd be able to get back to sleep or whether I should get up and have a snack. I was hungry, and I could never sleep when I was hungry. I tried to push thoughts of food from my mind and concentrate on what JenniFur had said. "But what about the 1080?"

JenniFur nodded. "Yes, Rufus was murdered elsewhere of course, so the murderer dragged his body here, hit him over the head, and slipped the bottle of poison into your laundry room to implicate you."

"But the murderer would have already had the 1080 poison. The murderer already intended to murder him with 1080. The murderer wouldn't have known that my husband works for the Office of Environment and Heritage. No, that doesn't make sense at all."

JenniFur stood up and arched her back. "It makes perfect sense. What part doesn't make sense?"

"It makes no sense because of the time frame. You yourself said that the murderer seized the moment. Nobody knew Rufus would yell at me in front of a lot of people. You said the murderer seized the opportunity to frame me for the murder. Sure, that part makes sense, but what doesn't make sense is the 1080."

JenniFur hissed. "How so?"

"Clearly, the murderer already had the 1080. It's not easy to get. My husband works for the

Office of Environment and Heritage sure, but the murderer had no way of knowing that before they bought the 1080."

JenniFur nodded slowly. "I see what you mean. That means it was a happy coincidence, seven degrees of separation and all that."

Now I was even more confused, and the late hour wasn't helping. "I don't know what you mean."

"Everybody would have a connection to somebody who works for the Office of Environment and Heritage," JenniFur said. "I mean, when I was a human, I knew the aunt of a famous Hollywood actress. Everyone is connected to someone in ways they might not even realise. Of course, the murderer had no idea that your husband works for the Office of Environment and Heritage. Like I said, that was probably a happy coincidence for them."

I sighed long and hard. "Then tell that to the police."

"The police won't be able to bring a charge against you without any evidence," JenniFur said. "Still, to be on the safe side, I think we need to solve the murder. If you ask me, Rufus was hit over the head post-mortem to make it look like you were the one who killed him. I don't know if checking for 1080 is something that routinely happens in an autopsy, but I expect the murderer planted the bottle here as a backup. One thing is clear, the murderer is trying to frame you. Maybe the murderer will do something else, something to make you look even more guilty."

I jumped out of bed. Now I really did need a snack. I hoped I hadn't eaten all the chocolate rum balls. Maybe there was still one left in the packet. "What else could the murderer possibly do?"

JenniFur yawned widely. "How should I know? I think we need to solve this murder and solve it quickly. Where are you going?"

"I'm hungry."

"Aren't we all? I need to get back to sleep. Let's have a quick chat about the suspects before you get your snack."

I sat on the edge of the bed, resigned. "Okay then. I spoke to Prudence in the café, and she told me Rufus has a son. He might be the only heir. She had no idea if Rufus was very wealthy, but we need to find out. The son is a golf pro. He gives lessons, and she thinks he lives in Hope Island."

"And then there are the commercial tenants,"

the cat added. "People often came into the shop and complained to Edison about Rufus. He treated them unfairly. One of them is an eyebrow specialist."

"An eyebrow specialist?" I parroted. "What's that?"

JenniFur made a strange choking sound at the back of her throat, and for a moment I thought she was coughing up another furball. When the strange sound stopped, she said, "It's obvious you don't know what an eyebrow specialist is. Look at your eyebrows! When was the last time you had them done?"

My hand went to my left eyebrow. "Oh, you mean waxed and tinted? Not for years. I did have them threaded a year or two ago, but my husband said it made me look like a clown."

Again, the strange sound. "A good thing you got rid of him. No, she does eyebrow tattooing and eyebrow laminating. She had a terrible falling out with Rufus, but I don't know the details. You could get your eyebrows done and investigate her. Make sure you don't get the woman who works for her."

I nodded. "Okay, so the suspects we have are the son and the unfairly treated tenants, notably the eyebrow specialist. Have you heard any more gossip?"

JenniFur appeared to be thinking it over. "The victim moved to a new house last year."

"From Coffs Harbour?"

JenniFur shook her head. "No. He moved here to the mountain some years ago. His recent move was from one side of Wild Lime Mountain to the other, to a house with a good view of the coast. His new neighbours' plants grew over his border fence, so he poisoned them all. They also grew prize orchids and bromeliads. Apparently, they had a greenhouse near the fence, and the poison killed all their prize plants."

I gasped. "How horrible!"

JenniFur readily agreed. "They were furious. And although it all happened a year ago, they say revenge is a dish best served cold. The police won't look at them at all closely now, given it was a year ago." She held up her paw and made motions in the air. "The son, the heir. We need to find out if the motive was money. The motive might have been revenge, so we need to look at the tenants and his neighbours."

"And I don't suppose the motive was love," I said. "Was he having an affair?"

Another choking sound emanated from JenniFur's throat. "Not as far as I know, and I've been party to plenty of gossip in the bookshop. People speak freely in front of cats."

"Thanks for your help. I'm off to get a snack."

"All right then, make it quick because you will need plenty of sleep. Your investigation starts in the morning."

It was only when I reached the kitchen that I realised I'd had a long conversation with a cat and had thought nothing of it.

CHAPTER 11

It had been a pleasant morning. There were more customers than usual, according to Edison, and he said it was because people were curious about me. He had said that was because I was new in town, but I suspected the real reason was that they thought I had murdered Rufus.

Nevertheless, the sales had been good, and my spirits were high. What's more, there had been no sign of the detectives.

There was a lull in customers around lunchtime. "It usually gets quiet at midday because people go to all the cafés and restaurants on the mountain," Edison told me.

We sat down at the table in the centre of the

shop. JenniFur appeared, purring loudly. "Did you hear any gossip today?" I asked her.

She rubbed her head against my leg. "Yes, I did."

I waited, and when she didn't say anything further, I asked, "Like what?"

"All sorts of things. Mainly, people say you seem nice, and some wondered if you murdered Rufus."

I pulled a face. "You didn't overhear anything that would help us solve the murder?"

"No."

"What did she say?" Edison asked me.

I repeated everything JenniFur had said. "Edison, tell me everything you know about Rufus. There must be some sort of a clue."

Edison shut his eyes tightly. "He does have a son," he began, but I held up one hand, palm outwards, to forestall him.

"Yes, Prudence and JenniFur have told me about the son who is the heir, the unfairly treated tenants particularly the eyebrow specialist, and his next-door neighbours whose plants he poisoned. Is there anybody else who might have wanted to murder him?"

Edison shrugged one shoulder. "I don't really

know, to be honest. The son did change his surname to his mother's maiden name."

"So no love lost between father and son, I guess?"

Edison continued to shrug. "Possibly, but perhaps Rufus asked his son to change his name from Greaves. At any rate, I was up half the night trying to think of people who wanted to murder him. Rufus was most unpleasant, but people don't go around murdering others who are simply unpleasant to them."

I readily agreed. "What about his life? Tell me everything you know about him, absolutely everything."

Once more, Edison shut his eyes. He opened them just before he spoke. "Let me see. He moved to Wild Lime Mountain about ten years ago."

"Was he wealthy?"

Edison nodded. "Yes, therefore the son is a likely suspect. The police will look at him closely, of course."

I nodded too. Edison pushed on. "I don't know if Rufus was wealthy before his wife was murdered, but of course he was wealthy afterwards. She was a very wealthy woman."

"Hang on a moment!" I shrieked. "Why didn't you tell me his wife was murdered?"

"I have told you now," Edison said calmly.

"But what if he murdered her? You said she was wealthy."

JenniFur's whiskers twitched. "Or maybe the person who murdered her also murdered Rufus."

I rubbed my forehead. "But don't you see? This can't be a coincidence. His wife was murdered, and he was murdered."

Edison waved one finger at me. "But she was murdered over ten years ago. If somebody wanted to murder them both, they would have surely murdered him soon after they murdered her."

I thought it over. "What were the circumstances of her murder?"

"It was a home invasion gone wrong," Edison said. "Not that I know much about it. That's what people said when he first moved to town."

He stopped talking when a lady entered the shop. A cloud of expensive French perfume preceded her. She walked straight over to Edison. "Has my order come in yet?"

He shot her a wide smile. "Yes, it certainly has, Carol. I emailed you this morning."

She chuckled. "I didn't check my email."

They walked over to the counter where Edison produced a hardcover book. The lady clasped her hands with delight. He wrapped it, and she swiped her card. As soon as she was out of the door, I prompted him, "Go on."

Edison tapped the side of his head with his index finger. "Where was I? What was I saying?"

"You were telling me about the home invasion."

He nodded slowly. "Yes, a home invasion gone wrong. It was at night. Somebody broke in and stole all her jewellery. She was hit over the head in the process, a fatal blow."

"I wonder if Rufus did it," JenniFur said.

I repeated her words to Edison. "No, Rufus was at a conference in Sydney at the exact time she was murdered, and he was seen by plenty of people. Apparently, there were several robberies in the area at the time, although none of the others were violent."

"Did they ever catch who did it?" I asked him.

"Not as far as I know. She was very wealthy. As I said, I don't know if Rufus had been wealthy before he married her, but he was certainly wealthy when he moved here. He moved here just after she was murdered," he added as an apparent afterthought. "No doubt he wanted to get away from everything."

"It *is* strange that they never caught who did it," I said. "Maybe Rufus put out a hit on her. We'll have to see if she has any relatives, because maybe one of them killed him in revenge."

"It is certainly possible," Edison said. His tone held doubt.

I drummed my fingers on the table. "But surely they would have done that sooner. I mean, why wait ten years to get revenge?"

"Because he changed his name," Edison said. "That's what people were saying at the time. The real estate agent who sold him his house, the original house when he first moved here that is, said he'd changed his name after the murder because he didn't want anyone to connect him with the murder and ask him questions about his wife. The murder was all over the news at the time. He said he wanted anonymity."

"Maybe he did put out a hit on his wife and then changed his name, and it took her relatives a few years to discover his whereabouts," I said.

"That does sound logical," Edison agreed. "I'll try to find out if she had any relatives. And, if the police take me in for questioning again, I'll put that theory to them. I don't care if they think I'm silly—the main thing is to prompt them to look into those avenues."

I was encouraged. "That's a great idea. If they question me again, I'll tell them the same thing."

Another two women walked into the shop but headed to the nearest bookcase. Edison leant over to me and said in little more than a whisper, "But that might be a dead end, no pun intended. It might really have been a home invasion. Rufus might not have had anything to do with it."

I had no time to ponder that as one of the ladies walked over to me and handed me a leaflet. "Hi, I'm Alison Newton. You're Nell Darling, aren't you?"

"Yes, I am."

"You're just in time for the welcome to Wild Lime Mountain meeting. We have one every two months to welcome the new residents to town. It's held in the library." She tapped her finger on the piece of paper. "Will you be able to come tonight? It starts at seven."

I was about to think up an excuse, any excuse, but I thought it might be a good way to gather information. "I'd love to come," I said. "Is the library easy to find?"

She nodded vigorously. “Yes, it’s in the middle of the shops to the north of town. It’s on the main street. You can’t miss it.”

And she was right. Just before seven that night, I turned left off the main street and into the library parking area. All the shops were closed, and the parking area was almost full.

I hoped this wasn’t going to be a complete waste of time. A smiling woman greeted me at the door and then handed me a bunch of pamphlets. “Go ahead and take a seat,” she said.

I went to sit in the back row, but a man blocked my way and wasted no time speaking to me. “Come on now, we’re all friendly here. No sitting up in the back row like in church.”

I offered him a weak smile and sat in the second back row. We were already off to a bad start. A woman at the end of the row raised her eyebrows at me and smiled. Clearly, we shared the same opinion.

The first person to speak was a local politician. He talked highly of himself and his political party. No surprises there. I was drifting off to sleep when a lady introduced as the local Landcare representative took the stand. I wondered if she would know anything about 1080. I made a mental note to ask her.

Thankfully, the Landcare representative didn't speak for too long, and then someone representing the local golf club took the stand. He, at least, was interesting. He said it was a nine-hole golf course and that everybody was welcome. Maybe he knew the victim's son. I could ask questions of him as well. I was beginning to think this wasn't a waste of time, after all.

The next speaker gave a speech about tank water. He said that most people are accustomed to a town water supply. He warned us all not to use water too freely as all the water in Wild Lime Mountain came from rainwater tanks. He gave the name of several water companies that would deliver water if our tanks ran dry. The next person to speak was from the Rural Fire Brigade. He told us where the collecting place was in case bushfires threatened.

The speakers took about an hour, and then a man who didn't introduce himself stood up and told us we could all have tea and coffee.

When we walked to the back of the building, I saw the coffee was instant, so I grabbed a tea bag and filled a polystyrene cup with hot water. The woman next to me said hello. "Have you been here long?"

"Only a day or two," I said. "What about you?"

"I've been here almost two months," she said. "I missed the last welcome meeting. A neighbour kept telling me about it, so I thought I should come to one or I'd never hear the end of it."

I chuckled. "Some ladies came into the bookstore today and told me about it. I bought the bookstore."

She looked interested. "Oh really? It's a lovely bookshop. I go in there quite a lot."

A man pushed between us and grabbed a tea bag. I drifted away so I could talk to the golf man. He was talking to somebody else, so I waited at an appropriate distance. I didn't have to wait long. He looked up and saw me standing there. "I'm interested in having golf lessons," I said. "Do you have lessons here?"

He shook his head. "No, I'm afraid we don't. You have to go down the mountain. There are plenty of golf courses at the Gold Coast."

"That's a shame," I said.

The man standing next to him agreed. He stuck out his hand. "Hi, I'm Kevin Hegarty."

"I'm Nell Darling." The man from the golf club was already speaking to somebody else. "How long have you been here?" I asked Kevin.

"I moved here about two months ago," he said.

"Did you miss the last meeting?"

He appeared confused by my words. "No. Oh, I see what you mean. The welcome meeting. No, I came to this meeting to help Barry."

"Barry?"

He nodded his head towards the golf guy. "The president of the golf club."

"So, you're a keen golfer too?"

He nodded enthusiastically. "I sure am. It's a lovely club. Volunteers do everything; they're the groundskeepers, everything."

I forced a smile. "That's really good." I didn't know what else to say.

He stared at me a moment and then said, "I hope you don't think I'm rude, but aren't you the lady who bought the bookshop?" I nodded and was about to say something when he continued. "Isn't that where Rufus Rutherford's body was found?"

I was glad the subject had come around to the murder. Maybe I could find out something. "Yes, that's right. Actually, I'm the one who found the body."

The man's face flooded with sympathy. "Oh no, how awful for you. I saw him yelling at you about the parking spot. And it's all around town that he was murdered."

"Yes, that's what the police said," I admitted.

He edged closer to me. "But what on earth was he doing in your bookshop in the middle of the night? He was a wealthy man. It wasn't as if he wanted to steal books or steal your daily takings or anything like that."

I shrugged. "The police didn't exactly say so, but I got the impression they thought he was murdered and then taken to my shop."

The man's brow furrowed. "That doesn't make any sense."

I shrugged. "Did he have many enemies in town?"

The man popped a whole cupcake into his mouth and swallowed it quickly. "Yes, everyone in town hated him," he said scornfully. "Though they say you shouldn't speak ill of the dead." He appeared to be thinking over his words, as he presently added, "But I don't think you will find anybody who had a good word to say about him. Have the police arrested anybody yet?"

"Not as far as I know. If they have, they haven't told me."

"Well, you must be relieved not to be a suspect. You'd think you *would* be a suspect given that you found the body." He hesitated and then added, "I hope I haven't upset you."

"I don't know. I mean, you haven't upset me, but I don't know whether I'm a suspect or not." I smiled widely as I spoke. I wasn't about to admit I was, in fact, a suspect. I spotted the Landcare representative and excused myself so I could speak to her. "Hi, I'm Nell Darling."

"Hi. How long have you been in town?"

It seemed that was the standard question. "Only a day or two," I said. "I bought the bookshop."

Her cheeks flushed red. "Oh! You found the murder victim."

Once more, I was pleased the subject had come up. "Yes, that's right."

"Do the police have any suspects?"

"If they do, they haven't told me," I said. I decided to come straight to the point. "Could I ask you a confidential question please?"

She took me by my arm and led me over to the side of the building. She looked at me expectantly.

"This is confidential," I said again. "The police think Rufus was murdered with 1080 poison."

I judged her surprise as genuine. "But I heard he was hit over the head."

"It was both," I told her. "Since you're involved with Landcare, I thought you'd know about 1080."

"What did you want to know about it?"

"I was wondering how the murderer got some. Doesn't someone need a permit?"

"They certainly do." She stopped speaking as Kevin Hegarty and Barry walked past us. When they had rounded the corner, she spoke again. "People need to have a permit, but it's been around for decades and it's probably sitting on most farms."

"You're kidding!" It seemed JenniFur was correct. I added, "A friend of mine told me lots of deadly old poisons are sitting around in farms."

"I am afraid your friend is right."

"So, if he was, in fact, poisoned with 1080, that wouldn't be a huge clue to help the police?"

She shook her head. "No, not really. So many people have had access to it over the years. Haven't you ever driven past warning signs that say 1080 baits are on the property?"

I thought about it. "As a matter of fact, I have."

The first lady I had spoken to appeared by my side and took over the conversation. I smiled and nodded at intervals—probably the wrong intervals—while I was thinking about what I had learnt.

I looked around and jumped. Had that been my reflection in the library window? Or was somebody outside, watching? I decided it had been my reflection. Still, an eerie awareness settled over me, a knowledge that the murderer was very close indeed.

CHAPTER 12

JenniFur had convinced me to get my eyebrows done so I could question Penny Lane, the beauty therapist who specialised in eyebrows. Edison had agreed with JenniFur.

I wasn't so convinced but figured I didn't have much choice. Until a likely suspect manifested, the police were going to continue to turn their attention to me.

And so, I had booked the appointment. It was going to last for one hour and fifty minutes. That alone made me nervous, having a stranger poking around my face for such a long time. I was also concerned she would be judgemental when she saw my horribly uncared-for eyebrows. I also didn't know how to question her, but Edison and JenniFur had told me to play it by ear. Easy for them to say.

I had expected the beauty therapy clinic would be in the shopping area, but it was in a residential area. The house was very pretty, a charming wooden cottage fronted by a row of crimson bougainvilleas. It was difficult to park as the house was on a corner, and the street was uncharacteristically narrow for an Australian street. I drove up on the front lawn and parked.

When I had made the appointment, I had been told to wait in my car and she would text me when she was ready for me. She explained she didn't have a waiting room. At precisely nine, a text came through telling me that my therapist was ready for me.

I walked up along the front footpath, noting a broken flagstone at the top of the stairs which had been covered with electrical tape.

I turned left and knocked on the door. A smiling woman opened the door, and I at once felt at ease. I noticed her flawless skin and absolutely perfect eyebrows. "I'm Penny," she said. "You must be Nell."

I assured her that I was and followed her

inside. Surely that couldn't be her real name—unless her parents had been Beatles fans.

A little hallway opened onto a bigger room. It was quite a small room and once I turned in, I spotted an oil diffuser alternating with different colours and producing a delightful fragrance of lavender. Penny told me to lie down and she would be right back.

I lay there, tension gnawing away in my stomach. When Penny returned, she bent over me. I shut my eyes tightly. "I'm going to do face mapping now," she said and then fell silent.

I wondered what face mapping was, but I wasn't about to ask. I also wondered how I could bring up the subject of Rufus. I thought maybe I should start talking and hopefully, the opportunity would present itself.

Penny poked and prodded at my eyebrows. "Have you heard of hybrid tinting?"

I had to admit that I hadn't.

"Most eyebrow colouring is done simply with tints, whereas you can have a combination of hair dye that colours the skin as well as the eyebrows. It lasts much longer, but many people don't need it. Maybe I'll start with tinting, and on your next appointment we can see if it's lasting well and make the decision whether to swap to hybrid tinting."

"That sounds good." I was hoping she'd asked me how long I had been in town, but she seemed more interested in the types of tinting available for eyebrows and the types of wax available for waxing. She seemed particularly excited about eyebrow laminating, and the conversation soon turned to microblading eyebrows.

I thought I had better bring up the subject of murder. "I only arrived in town the other day," I told her. "I used to live in Port Macquarie." I thought I had better tie the subject to eyebrows, so quickly added, "My husband always refused to let me get my eyebrows done, which is why they're in such a state now. I divorced him and moved here."

"That's wonderful! Now you can get your eyebrows done on a regular basis." She poked my left eyebrow as she spoke.

"Yes, it's good to get my eyebrows done. Do you do facials?"

"No, we only do eyebrows at the moment, but I will do facials again soon."

"That's great. I need to do something for myself now that I'm divorced. I moved to Wild

Lime Mountain for a happier life, but I had been here less than a day when I found a dead body in the bookshop."

I expected her to gasp. As no reaction was forthcoming, I figured she must have known all the time that I was the bookstore owner. "How awful for you," she said, her tone even. "Do they know who did it?"

I went to shake my head but realised I was having my eyebrows laminated so I had better keep perfectly still. "No, and they don't even know why the victim was in my bookstore in the first place. Apparently, he was a wealthy man, so he had no need to rob my place. And I must have been in the house at the same time as the murderer."

She did gasp then. "You're kidding!"

"I found the body soon after he was hit over the head. The murderer wouldn't have had time to get far away by then."

"You're lucky you weren't hurt too."

"Yes, that's what I thought. The police took me in for questioning and asked me who would want to kill him, but I said I wouldn't know because I've just arrived in town."

Penny grunted. "Everybody who knew him

wanted to kill him." She hesitated and then added, "I don't think you'll find anyone with a good word to say about him. I used to rent a building from him in a very good position, opposite the bakery, but he put up the rent by a ridiculous percentage."

"Is that legal?" I asked her.

"No, it isn't," she said, "but how could I fight it? *He* was the wealthy one. It was either pay up or leave, so I left."

"So, your beauty salon hasn't always been in your house?"

She made a strange sound. "No, not at all. This is a recent thing. I'm having tradesmen in to have it remodelled, and then I can offer facials again and get my business back on track."

"Did he do that to other commercial tenants as well?" I asked her.

Again, the strange sound. "Yes, lots of tenants. There was a little New Age shop next to me—you know, selling crystals and incense and things like that—and there was also a cute little furniture shop on the other side of me, and Rufus increased all our rents. Mine was the biggest increase by far, but they both closed down too."

"They haven't gone anywhere else on the mountain?"

"No. And those places are still vacant. Rufus wasn't able to get any other tenants at those ridiculously high prices, so he must have been losing a lot of money."

"It seems counter-productive," I said. "Why would he get rid of paying tenants in order to have vacant commercial premises?"

"Because he was a nasty, evil man," she spat. "He was extremely spiteful, and he didn't care if he cut off his nose to spite his face, so to speak."

"Did he have other commercial businesses in town that he leased out?"

She hesitated before speaking. "I can't say for certain, to be honest, but he did own a bar at the far end of the main street, and I know he had other places as well. The bar is still open, although I know they had trouble with him, and I did hear the other tenants left as well when he increased the rents."

I made to say something else, but she pre-empted me. "And he was supposed to be responsible for the lawns outside my building, but he neglected them. In the end, the man from the furniture shop used to maintain them. It wasn't fair. Nothing about that man was fair."

"Do you think it's possible that one of his tenants murdered him?" *Like you?* I silently added.

This time, she hesitated a long time before answering. "Anything is possible, I suppose. And you say you don't know why he was in your shop? Was he coming to harm you?"

I gasped. "Why would he want to harm me?"

"People said he was screaming at you outside in the street the night before he died. That *was* you, wasn't it?"

"Yes, that was me," I admitted. "He said I had taken his parking spot, but why would he want to do me harm? He was the one yelling at me, not the other way around."

"He was a nasty man. It seems strange that he was in your bookstore, that's all."

I agreed with her. "It *is* strange. I don't own any expensive books, and at any rate, the motive wasn't money because he was a wealthy man. Maybe the murderer set up a meeting in my bookstore."

"But surely not in the middle of the night," she said.

I had to agree with her. "Yes, it's all very

strange, that's for sure. Do you have any suspects?"

"No, I can't imagine who it could be."

"Is there any talk around town? I mean, have people mentioned any names?"

This time, Penny was silent for a long interval, and I realised that my name had been mentioned as a suspect. She took a deep breath and let it out slowly before saying, "Not really. I mean, he did poison his neighbours' plants, but would somebody get murdered over that? Maybe his son killed him because he'll get all his money."

"Maybe," I said absently. I wished I had thought of better questions to ask her. Now I was no further along, unless you counted my soon-to-be nicely waxed and laminated eyebrows, of course.

I was lost in my thoughts when I realised she was still speaking. "Sorry, what did you say?"

"I said we're soon going to offer eyebrow microblading here too," she said. "However, lamination looks like it's going to work nicely for you."

"I don't particularly want my eyebrows microbladed," I said. "I've heard microblading is painful, all that tattooing with cuts instead of dots."

"Well, it's not pain free, that's for sure, and it hurts more for subsequent treatments as the microblading is done over scar tissue."

I shuddered. "I'm sticking to laminating as it doesn't hurt at all."

"Yes, it doesn't hurt because it's simply perming, eyebrow perming. The only thing is, you can't get your eyebrows wet for the first twenty-four hours."

I burst out laughing.

"No, really, you can't get them wet for the first twenty-four hours."

I hurried to reassure her. "I wasn't laughing at your words. I was laughing at that scene in *Legally Blonde*."

"I haven't seen that movie in years. What scene was that?"

"Where Elle solves the murder. The murderer's alibi was that she was washing her hair, but she'd just had it permed. That's how Elle solves the case. The murderer wouldn't have washed her hair immediately after it being permed."

Penny chuckled as well. "Yes, that's right. You

must keep your eyebrows dry for the first twenty-four hours."

I wasn't getting anywhere, so I thought I might as well be more direct. "Penny, I definitely didn't murder Rufus, but because I'm new to town, the police suspect me. It would really help me if you could give me a name I could tell them. Is there anybody you can think of who would want to murder him?"

"Well, I certainly didn't murder him, although I was absolutely furious with him. I can't speak for the other tenants, but I know they were just as angry as I was. Still, nobody would murder him over that, surely. I know his neighbours were very upset with him, and what about his son? I heard there was bad blood between them. I'm sorry I can't be of any more help."

An hour later, I left the salon with highly attractive eyebrows but no new information.

CHAPTER 13

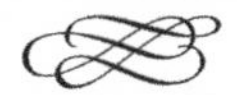

"I like your eyebrows," Edison said as soon as I entered the bookshop.

"Thanks." I looked around and asked in whispered tones, "Can anybody hear me?"

He shook his head. "Did you find out anything of interest?"

I let out a long sigh and rubbed my eyes with my left hand. "Not a thing. Penny Lane told me that Rufus had unfairly treated all his commercial tenants including two shops near her, and she told me about the neighbours with poisoned prize plants, and she told me about his son, the golf professional. I should book in for a lesson with him."

"Golf lessons?" exclaimed somebody.

I swung around to see a woman standing behind me. Another woman materialised behind her.

Edison made the introductions. "Nell, I'd like you to meet Daphne Dimples, and her twin sister, Delilah. Daphne and Delilah are good friends of mine. Ladies, this is Nell Darling, the new bookshop owner."

I cast my eye over them. Both were tall, but that was where the similarity ended. I guessed Daphne to be overly prim, the tightly buttoned blouse up to her neck covered in a demure, pale blue print, and her skirt falling to below her knees. Her shoes were sensible. Delilah, on the other hand, was wearing a fluorescent lime-green dress. It was shiny and sported enormous sleeves. Her sparkling pink cowboy boots completed the outfit.

"If you're wondering why we're both here at such an hour, I will have you know we shut the cakery at three every day," Daphne said, her tone uptight.

"I um, I wasn't wondering at all," I said honestly.

Delilah hurried forward and tapped my arm. "Please can we come with you? We have always wanted to have golf lessons, haven't we, Daphne!"

"If you say so, Delilah." Daphne's lips were pursed.

I scratched my head. I was wondering how to decline politely when JenniFur appeared. "Take them both, Nell. It won't look so suspicious."

"What do you mean?" I asked without thinking.

"I should have thought my words were patently clear," Daphne said haughtily.

I glared at JenniFur. She said, "If it gets around town that you're visiting suspects by yourself, the murderer might put two and two together and come after you. If, however, you take these two women with you it should help your cover."

I nodded slightly. "That's a good idea," I said looking at JenniFur and then transferring my gaze to Daphne and Delilah.

Daphne's eyes narrowed, but Delilah clasped her hands with delight and did a little dance on the spot. "I wonder if we still have our clubs, Daphne?"

I was surprised. "Clubs? Didn't you say you have never played golf before?"

"Maybe we did many decades ago," Delilah said, "but we have completely forgotten how to play. We would be quite hopeless these days. We've been wanting to take lessons, but we just haven't had the motivation. This is a wonderful opportunity."

I looked at Edison, and he shrugged ever so slightly. "Okay, I'll see if I can make a booking for the three of us with the golf professional. What time would suit you?"

"Do you plan to go today?" Daphne asked.

"Yes, if I can, but I don't know if he has any vacancies."

Daphne waved her hand at me as though she was shooing away a recalcitrant hen. "Well then, there's no time like the present. Why don't you call him now, then we won't waste all our time standing around making silly small talk."

I slipped through the door into my apartment to call the golf club. It was easy enough to find the golf shop's number, and the phone was answered straight away. "Good afternoon, this is Simon Smythe, golf professional at the Hopeful Hope Island Golf Club. How may I help you?"

I told him my name and that I wanted lessons for three people.

"What standard are you?"

"I'm a complete beginner," I said. "And I

think my friends are as well. We were hoping to come at your earliest opportunity."

"I have nothing booked for this afternoon," he said.

"Would I be able to book for an hour's time?" I asked him. "I live on Wild Lime Mountain, and I don't know how long it would take me to get there. I only moved to Queensland this week."

"Yes, that's fine. Come straight to the golf shop when you get here." He continued to give me directions from State Route 4 and told me where to park. It was only when he hung up, I realised I had forgotten to ask about the cost of the lessons. I had no doubt it was a rather posh golf club.

When I walked back out, Delilah said, "And don't you worry about the cost, Nell. It is very kind of you to take us, so we insist upon paying it."

I looked at Daphne who looked rather shocked at Delilah's pronouncement but said nothing. "Oh, I couldn't possibly," I began but Delilah took a step forward and held out her hand as though she was trying to stop a horse galloping at her. "Absolutely, I insist. Don't we, Daphne?"

She spun around to Daphne. "Yes, certainly,"

Daphne said, although her tone held no enthusiasm.

"Okay then, if you're sure. Thank you very much. He said we can have a lesson in an hour. How long will it take us to get there?"

"We should leave in fifteen minutes to be on the safe side," Daphne said. "I'd never like to arrive anywhere late. Arriving late is a sign of constipation."

I was certain I had heard her wrongly. "I'm sorry, what did you say?"

Daphne looked down her long nose at me. "Why are you sorry?"

"Did you say constipation causes lateness?"

Daphne drew herself up to her full height. "I most certainly did not! I said being late is a sign of constipation. The two go hand-in-hand, you see."

"I see," I said, although I most certainly didn't.

"Well, we had better go and get ready and put on some golf clothes," Delilah said. "We'll meet you back here in fifteen minutes, Nell?"

"Yes, that would be good."

As soon as they were out of earshot, I turned to Edison. "Now, where were we? I was telling you about Penny Lane, the eyebrow lady."

"Do you think she did it?" Edison asked me.

"She seems too nice, to be honest." I tapped my chin. "And she seems so slender that I wouldn't think she'd have the strength to knock somebody over the head."

Edison waved his index finger at me. "You forget, the victim was poisoned and possibly hit over the head post-mortem, no doubt when he had already succumbed to the poison. That wouldn't take any strength."

"But dragging the body into my shop would have taken strength," I pointed out.

Edison nodded. "But your intuition didn't prompt you to suspect her?"

"No, but it hasn't prompted me to suspect anybody at all," I admitted. "This son looks like the prime suspect, at any rate. He inherits everything, and that's a good motive for murder."

Edison readily agreed. "It certainly *is* a good motive for murder. The police would be aware of that as well. Have you heard from them at all today?"

"No, not since I had my eyebrows done. Have you?"

He shook his head and smiled. "No, so maybe they are looking into the other suspects."

"I certainly hope so. I had better go and find something to wear to golf."

I went to my bedroom with the intention of looking through my clothes but then did a quick Internet search on my phone first. I didn't have any golf shoes, but the search stated that I needed to wear sensible shoes with no spikes, and there were plenty of rules about what women could and couldn't wear. Luckily, I found the right sort of shirt to wear. As I was a football fan, I also had a Brisbane Lions cap that would protect me from the sun. Even though it was late in the day, it was Queensland, and sun protection was always necessary.

I walked back downstairs just in time to hear the cat gasp. Edison's gasp followed soon after.

Daphne and Delilah had returned to the bookstore. Daphne was wearing sensible clothes, long cream pants with a matching cream blouse buttoned all the way up, whereas Delilah looked like something out of a sixties movie. Her trousers were sky blue with big yellow daisies embroidered all over them. Stranger still was her tight tank top in a vivid shade of red, the fluorescent green bias binding forming a strange zigzag pattern over it. I hadn't seen anything so bad since my last migraine.

But that was not what caught my attention. Delilah was wearing a tinfoil hat. "Is that some sort of sun protection?" I asked her hesitantly, wondering whether I should say anything at all or whether I should keep my mouth shut.

Delilah laughed uproariously. "Sun protection? Of course not! It's the aliens."

Once more I thought my hearing had failed me. "Aliens?" I repeated. "Did you say aliens?"

"Yes, of course. There have been many sightings of UFOs over Hope Island. I have a spare tinfoil hat if you'd like to wear one. You wouldn't want to be abducted by aliens while on a golf course, would you?"

I had to admit that I wouldn't. "I wouldn't like to be abducted by aliens *anywhere,*" I said, "but I am quite happy with the hat I am currently wearing. Thanks so much all the same."

Delilah looked quite put out. "Why are you wearing a Brisbane Lions hat? Were you a supporter before you moved to Queensland?"

I nodded. 'Yes, I lived in Fitzroy in my youth and followed them then."

Delilah nodded sagely. "Ah yes, and Fitzroy

club became Brisbane club many years ago. Oh, no offence, Nell. You're half our age."

"Not half, Delilah," Daphne snapped. "We're not much over eighty."

I smiled and studied Delilah's hat. It looked as though it was made from aluminium foil, and two antennae stuck out from it. She looked entirely like the Martian from the old reruns of *My Favorite Martian* I had seen the previous week. I collected my thoughts. "We might as well be on our way."

"I will never understand all this nonsense about aliens," Daphne grumbled. "But then, *I* am the sensible one."

I opened the door of the bookstore and barrelled straight into somebody. "I'm sorry," I said, but then my breath caught in my throat. It was Detective Caspian Cole.

CHAPTER 14

The detective's face was bright red. "I'm terribly sorry. I was in a hurry," he said, stating the obvious.

I stepped aside to let him into the shop and then followed him inside. "So was I," I admitted. "Did you want to question me again?"

I looked up to see the sisters staring at him in horror. When Detective Cole saw them, his eyes widened. The three of them nodded to each other, and each took a step backwards. It was clear they knew each other, and there was something else going on. I thought it even more peculiar given the fact the detective lived in Wild Lime Mountain.

Daphne, keeping an eye on the detective,

walked over to me. "We'll wait for you in our shop," she said. "Come to the cakery when you're ready. We'll put a closed sign on the door but will leave it open for you."

With that, the sisters took off at a speed that belied their age, with Delilah looking back over her shoulder at the detective as they left. They were certainly uncomfortable with him.

He seemed to take a moment to recover. "No, I'm not here to question you. I need to buy a book."

"What sort of book?" I asked without thinking.

The detective appeared uncomfortable. "I want to look through your technical section. I'm looking for reference material."

I was puzzled. "Reference material? Wouldn't the Internet be better?"

The cat ran between my legs, nearly tripping me over. "Some bookshop owner you are!" she spat. "You need people to buy books—physical books. Don't discourage customers!"

"I don't really like the Internet," the detective admitted. "I like the feel of a proper book."

"Oh, I see." I turned to Edison. "Where's the technical section?"

"I'll show him where it is," Edison said.

The detective followed Edison, presumably to the technical section. As he lived locally, why had Edison looked so surprised to see him the other day? Or rather, he had looked alarmed or discomfited. And now the sisters looked that way as well. Were the three of them engaging in some illegal activity and feeling guilty when they saw the detective? I had no idea. My mind ran through the possibilities—counterfeit ring, bank robbery, scammers, and other criminal activities.

Edison's words broke me out of my reverie. "Shouldn't you go to your golf lesson?"

I chuckled. "I almost forgot about that." I lowered my voice and added, "I got such a fright to see the detective. I thought he might be here to arrest me or at least question me again."

"I will go and see what books he's looking at," JenniFur said before running after the detective, her tail fluffed up to the maximum.

I walked the short distance to the cakery. I had not really noticed it before. The architecture suggested an everyday shop front, wood with wide glass windows. That was where the ordinary and everyday ended.

Above the windows in a flowing script were

the words, *Lamington Lane Cakery*. The left side of the name was pale blue with tiny roses painted over it. Strangely, there was a line down the middle, and the other side of the wording was black with distorted faces painted on the lettering. It took me a moment or two to realise they were meant to be alien faces.

I walked over to the door which was set in a little from the front of the building. Glass cabinets lined both sides of the door. To my left were pretty cupcakes as well as custard tarts and lemon meringue pies. My mouth watered. To the right of the door, the glass cabinets were lined with what could easily have been Halloween decorations, although instead of orange, they were mainly black, white, and a strange shade of green. Some of the cupcakes had alien faces complete with antennae.

I tried the old brass door handle, and to my relief it did, in fact, open. I pushed it and stepped inside. Starting from the middle of the doorway, and running the length of the shop, was a black line. Alien decor abounded to the right of me, yet to the left, it could easily have been a quaint English tea room. I schooled my features into a neutral expression to hide my shock and continued to the counter where the sisters were standing, apparently doing some paperwork. The counter was likewise split in half and decorated strangely.

Delilah looked up at me. "You didn't take long," she said. "That's good, we won't be late."

"And therefore no one will think we're constipated," I said automatically and then immediately regretted it when Daphne shot me a cold look.

Soon, we were in the car driving down the mountain. Delilah was happy to talk, whereas Daphne barely said a word.

When I got to the bottom of the mountain, Daphne did speak, to guide me over the overpass which was the labyrinth of lanes over the M1. I would never have been able to figure out the way by myself. There were five sets of traffic lights in close succession, and then the road opened somewhat.

"It's not too far now," Delilah said. "You turn off before we reach Sanctuary Cove."

"Honestly, Delilah, your directions are completely useless," Daphne said waspishly. "Nell has never been to Sanctuary Cove, so how on earth would she know to turn off before it?"

"My directions are not useless," Delilah snapped. "Have you ever heard of *signs,* Daphne? Signs? Big green signs by the side of the road? If Nell goes past a sign that says Sanctuary Cove, she will know she has gone too far."

Daphne muttered something to herself. I was grateful she didn't say it aloud.

To cut off the argument before it progressed, I said, "It seems as though we are approaching a golf course now."

"No, that's another Hope Island golf course," Delilah said. "They have several. We're coming up to a big roundabout, and you are to turn there."

Thankfully, the rest of the drive continued without incident. I found the golf course without any trouble and parked in the parking area. We got out of my car. I locked it, and we continued down the small concrete path, with the golf club on our right, to the shop.

A man, I presumed Simon Smythe, was standing behind the desk. He looked up and smiled at us. It was a thin-lipped smile, and my first impression was that he was mean. Still, that might have been because he looked so much like his father. There was certainly a strong family resemblance.

"Hello, can I help you ladies?"

I walked over to the desk. "Hi, I'm Nell Darling and these are my friends, Daphne and Delilah Dimples. We booked a beginner lesson with you."

His smile widened. "Certainly. So, none of you have had any experience?"

We all shook our heads.

"All right then, let me get you some golf clubs." He cast around for a while, finding us golf clubs the correct length and then said, "Follow me. We will find a nice, quiet spot. I'll drive the golf buggy and you ladies can follow."

"I will drive," Daphne said quite firmly.

He peered at her. "Do you think you can keep up, dear?" Before waiting for a response, he walked outside and hopped in a golf buggy.

I could not help but notice that Delilah's face had turned white. "But Daphne, you were disqualified from driving."

Daphne narrowed her eyes. "What nonsense, Delilah! You do not need a driver's licence to drive a golf cart. It's perfectly legal for me to drive this."

"That's not what I'm afraid of," Delilah said. Still, she climbed in beside Daphne who was already sitting in the driver's seat, and I climbed in behind them.

I had one leg in and the other still on the ground when Daphne took off, flinging me backwards. I nearly fell out of the golf cart.

"Could you slow down a bit?" Delilah asked her.

"Weeeeee!" was Daphne's only reply.

For a prim, uptight woman, Daphne was certainly turning into a Jekyll and Hyde.

I breathed a huge sigh of relief when Daphne finally brought the cart to a stop.

"The man wants you to back up," Delilah told her. "You've gone too far. You're on the green."

Daphne snorted and put the cart into reverse.

I heard a loud scream and looked behind me. Daphne had reversed the car over Simon Smythe's foot. "My foot, my foot!" he screamed.

"You parked on his foot!" Delilah yelled.

"Why are you always stating the obvious, Delilah?" Daphne snapped. "I can't work under pressure." She accelerated, and the golf cart lurched forward.

I jumped out of it and hurried over to the golf pro. "Are you all right?"

"Sure, sure." He waved at Daphne. "Just leave it there. It's in the wrong place, but please don't try to move it."

Daphne narrowed her eyes. "I did indeed keep up with you, Mr Smythe."

He shot her a glare. "All of you, please call me Simon. First of all, I will show you how to putt."

He demonstrated how far apart we should put our feet and how to hold the golf club. He seemed in a rather bad mood—who could blame him?—and I wondered how to bring the subject around to his father.

"I am terribly sorry about your father," I said, deciding on the not-so-subtle route.

He stood upright and stared at me. "Did you know him?"

"I only moved to Wild Lime Mountain the other day." I avoided answering his question. "The whole town is talking about it."

He bent over his putter again. "I bet they are," he muttered.

I didn't know what else to say. Maybe I should have thought this through a little better. I could hardly ask him if he murdered his father. "Are you the only child?"

Once more, he stood up and looked at me. "Yes, what of it?"

"I was going to ask you to pass on my condolences to the rest of your family."

"There *is* no rest of my family," he said. "Now, you try it."

Despite his obvious anger issues, he was quite a good teacher. The three of us were soon managing to putt quite well. Still, I hadn't made any inroads into the investigation. I consoled myself with the fact I had discovered he was the only heir.

After the lesson progressed and Simon had shown us all how to do a proper swing, I figured I should question him some more. But to say what? The funeral! That was it.

To Simon, I said, "Is the funeral open to everybody? We would like to attend."

I held my breath, wondering whether Daphne or Delilah would disagree with me, but thankfully they remained silent.

He looked up from his driver. "Sure, it's tomorrow morning. The police released the body today. I want to put this all behind me, so I decided to have the funeral tomorrow."

"That wouldn't have given you much time to organise it."

"It was already organised," he said. "The police had given me the heads up about when they would release the body, and the funeral directors were quite helpful."

"We'd love to come and pay our respects unless you would have any objections," I continued.

He looked surprised. "Why would I have any objections? The service is going to be held at Carrara, and he'll be buried there. You're more than welcome to come."

I thanked him. He was an unpleasant person, but that didn't mean he was the murderer. There were plenty of unpleasant, non-murdering people in the world.

Still, he had the most to gain, as far as I knew. That is, if the motive for murder was money. Maybe it was revenge. I would have to question the plant loving neighbours. I hoped I would get an opportunity to do so at the funeral.

The lesson drew to an end. "I will drive you

all back," he said. "Leave that other gold golf cart here."

"I'm happy to drive it," Daphne said.

"No!" His exclamation was so loud that we all jumped a little. Daphne did not say a word but climbed into the front seat next to him. Delilah and I climbed in the back, despite there only being room for one.

When I got into my own car, I made a mental note never to let Daphne drive. "I think I can find my way back," I told the sisters. "It seems fairly straightforward."

"So, do you think he did it?" Delilah asked me.

I was taken aback. "Did what?"

"Why, murdered his father, of course."

Daphne piped up. "Yes, that's obviously why you had a golf lesson with the son, the only heir. You are doing a spot of investigating."

I chuckled. "I didn't realise I was so obvious."

"Only to us," Delilah said. "Maybe not to normal people."

I wondered what she meant by that, but figured it probably had something to do with aliens, so I didn't like to ask.

Delilah spoke again. "I found it rather strange that he said *the* body rather than *his* body."

"It's just a figure of speech, Delilah," Daphne snapped.

"You're a linguist all of a sudden are you, Daphne? I, for one, did find it very strange. It sounds like he didn't like his father."

"Maybe not," Daphne said, "but that doesn't make him a murderer. Nobody else liked his father, as far as I know."

As the sisters bickered, I continued my drive up the mountain thinking about Simon Smythe. Had he, in fact, murdered his father? And if so, why did he murder him in my shop?

I was running out of suspects. I had already spoken to Penny Lane and now Simon Smythe, and unless it was another unfairly treated tenant, I only had the plant loving neighbours left to question. That is, of course, unless Rufus's murder was connected in some way with the murder of his wife.

A feeling of dread settled over me.

CHAPTER 15

I awoke the next morning to the sound of heavy rain. I staggered out of bed, wrapped my bathrobe around me, and staggered to the window. I was not a morning person.

Sure enough, the sky was dark and gloomy. I went in search of coffee. I hadn't gone far when JenniFur nearly tripped me down the stairs. "Why did you run between my legs like that?" I asked her, my tone none too kindly.

"I'm a cat, remember? That's what we do." With that, she hissed and ran down the stairs. I followed her down the stairs and was about to go into the kitchen when I heard a terrible scratching sound at my front door. I walked over and opened it for JenniFur. She stuck her head outside, but her body remained inside. "Are you going to go out?" I asked her.

There was no response. I tried to close the door gently to encourage her to put her head back in, but instead, she moved forward a little more so that half of her was now outside and half was inside. "It's raining," she said.

"Yes, are you going in or out?"

Again, there was no response. I was debating whether to leave the door open—not the best idea with the murderer on the loose—when JenniFur ducked back inside. I breathed a sigh of relief and shut the door. As soon as I did, JenniFur scratched on the door. "I want to go out," she said.

I threw my hands in the air. I opened it again, and once more she poked her head through the door. She would not move.

I gave up. Murderers or no murderers, I needed my coffee, and I wasn't going to play the game of inside and outside with the cat. I threw caution to the wind, left the door open, and hurried to the coffee machine.

I was sitting at the kitchen table, sipping my coffee and looking out the window at the driving rain, when JenniFur came back in, shaking herself. Little droplets of water flew over the room.

I hurried to shut the door and then returned to my seat. JenniFur shook herself again and then said, "When you came back last night, I forgot to tell you about the book the very handsome and most eligible bachelor, Detective Cole, bought."

"I already know," I informed her. "Edison told me."

"What exactly did he say?"

I waved one hand at her in dismissal. "I can't remember the exact name, but it was something to do with poisons."

JenniFur nodded. "That's right. It was called *Forensics Toxicology: Methods and Applications*. He was looking for information about 1080, of course."

"It is weird that he didn't do an Internet search like anyone else would," I said, half to myself.

JenniFur vehemently disagreed. "I think it's a very attractive quality in a human man. He has nice shoulders too. It's a shame he shaves off his whiskers."

I rubbed my forehead. It was too early in the day for this conversation. Actually, any time of day would have been wrong for this conversation.

I did the only thing I could do; I popped in another coffee pod.

"So, what are your investigative plans for today?"

I looked at JenniFur. "I'm going to Rufus's funeral later today, but I'm going to spend the morning learning about the shop. I need to know about running the place. There's a lot more to it than knowing how to work the till, you understand. Oh, and JenniFur, I've been meaning to mention the secret room."

JenniFur had been licking her paw and rubbing it over her ears, but her paw froze in mid-air. "Whatever do you mean?"

"The secret room. I saw a door in the wall of the corridor that leads to the back of the shop. I'm absolutely certain I saw a door there once or twice, but when I went back to the very same place later, there was no door."

"Had you been drinking?"

I narrowed my eyes, but then remembered that cats narrow their eyes when they're happy, so I made an effort to open my eyes as wide as I could to show my displeasure. "No, I hadn't been drinking. I was positive I saw a door there, and when I went back it was a solid wall."

"You're not making any sense." With that, JenniFur ran out of the room.

Well, she was no help. I had a leisurely breakfast of Vegemite and peanut butter toast and another two cups of coffee before having a shower and getting dressed. I walked back down to the bookstore, thrilled that I owned it. I walked along, running my hands over the books, before sitting in a comfortable chair in one of the reading nooks and looking around the room. After an interval, I walked back to where I had seen the door.

The wall shimmered for a brief second—was I getting a migraine?—but then was solid once more. This was all too strange. I was certain I had seen the door there previously. I was still staring at the wall when Edison came into the bookshop. "Are there things I don't know about the bookshop?" I said by way of greeting.

Edison nodded. "Yes, I'll show you how to do the ordering now."

That wasn't what I had meant. Since JenniFur had once been human, it occurred to me that there might be a not-quite natural explanation for me seeing a door that was no longer there, but I didn't want to press Edison on it, not quite yet.

The morning passed uneventfully. Edison

introduced me to some regular customers, and there were plenty of tourists in the shop as well. The tourists were interested in buying the classics.

When it was time to go to the funeral, trepidation settled over me. "What's wrong?" Edison said. "You look as though you've seen a ghost."

"Yes, I do feel anxious. My stomach's churning. I think it's because the murderer will be at the funeral."

Edison raised one bushy, white eyebrow. "I am not sure I get your meaning."

"Murderers always go to funerals," I told him. "Haven't you ever seen *Midsomer Murders*? The detectives always go to funerals because they know the murderer will be there."

Edison's brow furrowed deeply. "Then it doesn't seem a very wise thing for the murderer to do, to attend the victim's funeral."

I agreed. "Maybe it *is* necessary if the murderer is a close relative."

Edison picked up a book, mumbled to himself, and put it in a different section of the store. "Yes, but if someone *is* a murderer and doesn't actually have to be at the funeral, then it is quite the silly thing to do because the police will be there, like you said."

"Yes," I said absently. "I haven't met the plant loving neighbours yet. What are their names? And what do they look like? I am sure they won't be wearing shirts with 'plant loving neighbours' written all over it."

Edison chuckled. "Nick Northey and Atticus Aldridge. Atticus is tall and thin, whereas Nick is short and round. They're both very friendly."

"Too friendly to murder somebody?"

Edison shrugged. "Maybe, maybe not, but they didn't do it. Nell, I'm worried about you going to that funeral. I know the police suspect you, but shouldn't you leave it to them to investigate?"

I narrowed my eyes and put my hands on my hips. "Did Detective Cole say something to you about me investigating?"

Edison became flustered. "Err, um, he might have," he sputtered.

"What did he say exactly?"

"He said he was concerned that you would investigate because you thought you were a suspect."

"I *am* a suspect."

"Don't shoot the messenger."

I thought it over. "So, you don't mind looking after the bookshop while I go to the funeral? I feel bad—I've been investigating the murder and leaving you to mind the shop."

"I don't mind at all," Edison assured me. "You won't be much help until you learn the ropes anyway."

"And I won't learn the ropes while I'm off trying to solve a murder either."

Edison pursed his lips and nodded. "Still, is there anyone else to investigate?"

I shook my head. "The way I see it, it was either the son, Simon Smythe, or the unfairly treated eyebrow specialist, Penny Lane, or the plant loving neighbours. What were their names again? Neil something?"

"Nick Northey and Atticus Aldridge," Edison supplied.

I nodded. "Yes, them. Still, I can't help thinking that the victim's murder was somehow connected with his wife's murder ten years ago."

Edison pulled up the blind in the front window and peered outside. "Goodness me, this rain is still coming down hard. So, you think

Rufus murdered his wife, and somebody murdered him in revenge?"

"Yes."

JenniFur strolled into the room. "You forgot to tell her, didn't you?" She addressed the remark to Edison, but, of course, he couldn't hear her.

"JenniFur says you have forgotten to tell me something."

"Forgot?" Edison looked blank and then slapped himself on the forehead. "Oh yes, silly me! How could I have forgotten?"

"What is it?" I prompted him.

"When the detective left yesterday, I did a lot of research on the Internet, and as far as I could tell, Rufus's wife didn't have any living relatives. Her parents had died in an accident some years before. They were very wealthy, and that's where she got her money, you see."

"And she didn't have any siblings? Aunts, uncles, cousins?"

Edison shook his head. "No, I found some old news articles about her murder. They said she was the only surviving child of her parents."

"But she could have had a cousin or…" I would have said more, but Edison interrupted me.

"No, I can't remember everything the article

said, but she had no living relatives. I'll find it again and show you."

I waved one hand at him. "No, that's okay. What about a close friend? Or maybe a lover? Maybe she was having an affair. That certainly wouldn't have been in the newspapers."

Edison peered at me over the top of his glasses. It was the first time I realised he wore glasses. My lack of observation skills certainly didn't bode well for me as an amateur sleuth. "That's a good point, but I'm afraid we will have no way of finding out."

"Then it looks as though we have come to a dead end, at least in pursuing that avenue of investigation."

The door opened, and in breezed Delilah, followed by Daphne. Daphne was dressed all in black, looking for all the world like someone in mourning clothes straight out of Victorian times, whereas Delilah was wearing a rather too short skirt in a bright red fabric, and her blouse sported gigantic sleeves. Half of the blouse was sky blue, and the other was pastel pink. Big wooden buttons completed the picture.

Daphne was wearing a small black fascinator,

but Delilah's hat was huge and straw, with artificial flowers pinned around the brim.

Delilah thrust a plate at me. "I made these for the funeral," she said. "For the Wake."

I looked down and gasped.

CHAPTER 16

"What are those?" I squealed.

"Aren't they delightful?" A wide smile broke out on Delilah's face. "I made them especially for the funeral. They're coffin cupcakes."

"Coffin cupcakes?" I repeated in horror.

I could scarcely believe my eyes. The cupcakes were indeed in the shape of coffins and were brown in colour—I assumed chocolate icing. "They're very detailed," I said when I managed to find my voice.

Delilah beamed from ear to ear. "Thank you!"

Daphne elbowed her in her ribs. "I don't think that was a compliment. They are in poor taste."

"Poor taste? What do you mean? All my cupcakes taste delightful. Everybody says so."

Daphne rolled her eyes.

Delilah nodded to the big tray Daphne was carrying. "Show them what else I made!"

Daphne rolled her eyes again and took the lid off the cloche.

I gasped, more loudly this time. I had thought nothing could be worse than the coffin cupcakes, but there, sitting on a silver tray, was a large green and black cake in the shape of a skull.

"What, what, what is it?" I stammered.

Delilah's eyebrows met in the middle, forming a unibrow. "Why, it's a skull cake, of course."

"That is most inappropriate," Daphne said in scolding tones.

"Not at all." Delilah narrowed her eyes. "I've made it look like an alien skull. It doesn't look like Rufus at all. Now *that* would have been inappropriate."

I left them bickering and went to fetch my car keys and handbag.

I managed to find my way to the cemetery through Gold Coast traffic easily enough with the help of Daphne and Delilah, who insisted on coming with me. JenniFur had wanted to come with me too, but I had told her that cats were not allowed in cemeteries. She had complained loudly and at length.

The cemetery was picturesque and pretty, with huge beds of different types of gardens.

I drove down a hill and found a parking spot easily enough. We all climbed out of the car. I spotted several people making their way into a building opposite the café. "They must be going to the funeral," I said.

And I was right. We walked into the Chapel, a large room painted in tones of white and pale grey with huge picture windows overlooking tropical gardens. We took our seats near the back. Daphne whispered something to Delilah, who turned to me and dug her long, bony fingers into my arm. "Look at the coffin," she hissed.

I did so. It looked like any other coffin to me. "Why, what of it?"

"It looks cheap," she said. "I'm going to get a closer look."

She half rose, but Daphne grabbed her arm and pulled her back to her seat. She landed with a thud. "What is it, Daphne?"

"You can't look at the coffin, Delilah. It's a closed casket funeral."

Delilah stood back up. "So, arrest me!" With that, she squeezed past me and hurried down the aisle towards the coffin.

I craned my neck to look. It was a wooden coffin. It didn't look particularly cheap to me, but then again, I wouldn't have a clue. I watched as Delilah bent over, looking at the coffin and dabbing at her eyes.

When she returned, she squeezed past me once more and then said quite smugly, "I was right. It is definitely a cheap coffin. The son didn't waste any money on his father."

"But that doesn't make him any more of a suspect," I said.

"Nell is right," Daphne said, surprising me by agreeing with me. "Maybe he hated his father, but that doesn't mean he committed the murder."

Delilah pursed her lips. "Still, it is evidence."

She opened her mouth, and I was waiting for her to say more when there was a commotion down the front. I looked up to see Simon Smythe trying to pull something off the top of the coffin, and one of the funeral directors was trying to stop him.

"My father was in a Pentecostal Church that didn't believe in crosses," he yelled. "He wasn't

Catholic." He became agitated, waving his hands in the air. Once more, he reached for the cross on top of the coffin and tried to pull it off.

"How strange," Delilah said loudly. "Plenty of non-Catholic Christian religions have crosses."

Simon turned to glare at her before turning back to the coffin. "Get it off!" he wailed. "My father didn't want it there."

"We can give it to you after the service," the funeral director said.

Simon became even more agitated, and it took a bunch of the attendants to get him out of the room.

"See, he obviously did care about his father." I addressed my remark to Delilah.

She was having none of it. "Maybe they were charging extra for the cross. He's a penny pincher, that one." She held up her left hand, palm outwards. "I know, I know. You are about to tell me that all penny pinchers aren't murderers."

"Hush, Delilah." Daphne rounded on her sister. "This is a chapel. We need to be quiet. Besides, the murderer will be attending the funeral. Look, the detectives are here now."

I swung around. My stomach clenched when I

locked eyes with Detective Cole. I looked away at once.

Someone, I assume the minister, took the stand and welcomed everybody. He read from a piece of paper, saying what a lovely person the deceased had been and how he was now spending eternity in a better place. He then read a bunch of Scriptures slowly and in a monotone.

I was drifting off to sleep when Delilah elbowed me. "The suspect is going to say something now."

I rubbed my eyes and sat up straight. Sure enough, Simon Smythe was making his way to the pulpit. "My father was a hard man," he began, and after that inauspicious opening, he went on to extol the virtues—real or imagined, but I suspect imagined—of his father.

"If he's not a murderer, at least we know he's a liar," Delilah announced rather too loudly.

Several people turned around to look at her.

"Hush!" Daphne snapped.

Thankfully, Simon did not appear to hear. He spoke for at least five minutes and then sat down. The minister took the stand. "Would anyone else like to say something about Rufus?" He looked around expectantly.

Nobody spoke. The minister appeared quite disconcerted, and after an interval added, "Anybody?" His tone was hopeful. When nobody took him up on his offer, he sighed. "Refreshments are served in an anteroom." He gestured to his left. "Everyone is welcome."

With that, he walked down the long aisle. People followed him, starting from the front row. Daphne, Delilah, and I were amongst the last to leave. "The son can't be that stingy after all, if he's paying for refreshments," Delilah said.

The people walking past stared at her.

Daphne was clearly embarrassed. "Hush, Delilah. Everybody can hear you. You never speak; you yell."

"I do not yell," Delilah said in a booming voice. "And besides, they won't know what I'm talking about."

"They can't fail to know what you're talking about," Daphne said through clenched teeth. "Not only do you make it very clear, you yell it."

I thought I had better pre-empt any further argument. "Let's follow everyone into the anteroom now, and maybe we can have some coffee," I suggested.

"Coffee? It's always that instant stuff." Daphne screwed up her nose.

I rubbed my eyes. Still, they happily followed me into the room. I saw a big jar of instant coffee next to a huge urn of boiling water, so I skirted around it and came up behind a crowd of people all looking at something on a table. I squeezed past them to see the tray of Delilah's cupcakes.

Everyone was gasping and pointing to the coffin cupcakes and the large skull cake. Delilah hurried over. "I made them," she announced proudly. "The coffins are chocolate, and the skull is chocolate and peppermint."

The man standing next to her grabbed a coffin cupcake and shoved it into his mouth, but his wife took his arm and pulled him away from the table.

I wanted to make Delilah feel better. I picked up one and hesitantly nibbled a little bit of it. "Wow, it's really good," I said honestly.

"I might try one," said a voice beside me.

I turned around to see a man. I recognised him as the friend of the golf club president, but I couldn't remember his name. He was looking at me expectantly, obviously wanting me to introduce him to the sisters. "Hi there. Nice to see you again. These are my friends, Daphne and Delilah Dimples."

He didn't introduce himself but waited for me. What could I do? I had forgotten his name and didn't like to admit it. I pretended to cough. "There's something in my throat. Why don't you introduce yourself?" I turned away and pretended to cough harder. I turned back after he had introduced himself. Kevin Hegarty. That's right. I knew it started with K, but I would have guessed Ken. Thank goodness I hadn't introduced him as Ken.

Daphne looked him up and down. "I haven't seen you around before. Are you from Wild Lime Mountain?"

Kevin nodded vigorously. "I only arrived in town two months ago."

"And where did you come from? Somewhere in Queensland?"

He shook his head. "No, from Coffs Harbour, actually. It's halfway between Sydney and Brisbane, give or take a few hundred kilometres."

The sisters nodded. "Coffs Harbour is a beautiful place," Delilah said. "It has lovely beaches, some with beautiful names such as Sapphire Beach and Emerald Beach."

Kevin readily agreed. "I used to live just north of Sapphire Beach. It was an old house, with beautiful views. That was years ago, when I was married. After the divorce, I had to move to a much smaller place." His face flushed red.

"Have a cupcake," Delilah said in an obvious attempt to cheer him up.

It seemed to work. He popped half the coffin into his mouth in one go. "This is so good," he said after he swallowed his large mouthful.

"Daphne and Delilah run the Lamington Lane Cakery," I told him. "It's right near my bookshop."

"Yes, I know where it is," he said. "I'm supposed to be on a diet, but I have popped in there on occasion."

Delilah shot him a big smile. "Some people on diets have one cheat day a week. Maybe you could pop into our shop once a week."

"That sounds like the sort of diet I like," he said with a laugh.

I went into sleuth mode. "Were you a friend of the victim's?"

He shook his head. "Certainly not," he said with feeling. He looked around before he spoke. "I don't know many people in town, and I thought I should come to a social event. I need to make more friends. Barry, the golf club president, is always telling me I should get out and make new friends."

"That's a good idea," I said, but I doubted whether a funeral was indeed a place to make new friends. I kept my opinions to myself.

I had an uncanny feeling somebody was watching me. I turned around to see Detective Cole making his way towards me.

CHAPTER 17

Detective Caspian Cole stood in front of me, his hands on his hips. "Ms Darling, what are you doing here?"

I opened my mouth, but my words froze in my throat. Why did he always make me feel guilty? "My friends asked me to drive them here." I nodded to Daphne and Delilah. "Daphne has lost her licence, and they had no other way of getting here."

"What about an Uber?"

Was he serious? "That would be over two hundred dollars!" I exclaimed. "Surely, you weren't serious."

He crossed his arms over his well-muscled chest. Not that I was looking, mind you. "No, I wasn't serious, but my question remains, why are you really here?"

"They asked me to take them," I lied, hoping he wouldn't check, but then again, I was certain the sisters would be savvy enough to back me up.

"You said you didn't know anyone in town."

I narrowed my eyes. "Nobody knows anybody before they make their acquaintance."

"How philosophical of you, Ms Darling. Please leave the investigation to the professionals. I certainly hope I won't see you investigating."

"I hope you won't *see* me investigating either," I said.

He shot me a long hard look and then turned away, leaving me with an urge to stomp my foot. Instead, I muttered a grunt of frustration.

"Are you all right?"

I turned around to see a man standing behind me. "That detective irritated me," I said.

The men exchanged glances and then chuckled. One man was tall and slender, and the other man was short and round. I wondered if these were Nick Northey and Atticus Aldridge. "I take it you're a suspect in the murder of Rufus Rutherford too?" the short man asked.

"Yes, as a matter of fact, I am. I found the body."

The taller one leant forward. "Then you must be Nell Darling, the new owner of the bookstore."

"Yes, I am."

"I am Atticus, and this is Nick."

I smiled at them. "Yes, I've heard all about you." I thought I might as well cut straight to the point. "The victim poisoned your plants, and so you're suspects as well."

"Yes, we are," Nick said. "Although if we were going to poison him, we would have poisoned him sooner. Still, I expect the police think it was us because Rufus was murdered by poison. He poisoned our plants, so we poisoned him—at least that's what the police think."

My hand flew to my head. "That didn't even occur to me! But then again, it wasn't as if you would shoot him. None of us are on farms here."

Atticus nodded vigorously. "That's right, none of us have rifles to shoot the snakes, although I'm sure there are more snakes on Wild Lime Mountain than there are on farms."

Nick chuckled. "Have the police taken you in for questioning?"

"Yes, they have, and it was horrible. They made everything extremely innocent seem guilty."

"They took us in for questioning twice," Atticus said.

Nick nodded. "And the first time, they questioned us separately and then together. The second time, they questioned us separately. Both times, we were in one of those strange rooms with a one-way mirror. Or is it called a two-way mirror?" He looked at me as though I would know the answer.

I shrugged. "I think they can be called either. I have no idea, to be honest. Well, if you don't mind me saying so, it does make me feel a bit better that they questioned you twice. I thought I was the prime suspect."

Both men looked shocked. "But why would *you* be the prime suspect?" Nick asked me. "You had only just arrived in town, and you didn't know the victim."

"Yes, but try telling that to the police." I looked up and saw Detective Cole watching me.

Nick followed my gaze. "That cop is watching us now."

"He might be watching *me*," I admitted.

"That's why I was irritated just then. He told me not to investigate."

"You're investigating too?" Nick said with obvious delight. "Atticus and I have been putting our heads together ever since it happened, trying to find the killer."

Atticus chuckled. "Yes, that's why we made a point of speaking with you. We wanted to question you to see if you were the murderer."

I laughed too. "I wanted to speak to you two as well to see if you were the murderers."

Nick laughed loud and hard. When he recovered, he said, "Okay, it's out in the open. You can ask us whatever you like. But first, are you certain you didn't know the victim?"

"I am certain. The very day I arrived in Wild Lime Mountain, Rufus yelled at me and said I had taken his parking spot. Edison took me inside the bookshop. When I found the body in the early hours of the next morning, I didn't even know it was the same man, because it was dark, and he was lying face down."

"Then why do the police suspect you?" Nick asked me.

"Because he was poisoned with 1080 poison,

and my ex-husband works for the Office of Environment and Heritage."

I thought I would have to explain the connection, but Nick said, "Ah, yes! That's one of the organisations that can hand out permits for 1080."

I nodded. "My divorce was very nasty, but JenniFur,"—I caught myself just in time—"I mean, Edison, said the police might have thought my divorce was all a big pretence for the sole purpose of murdering Rufus. You see, I'm from Port Macquarie. Rufus used to live in Coffs Harbour, and my ex-husband's jurisdiction extends to Coffs Harbour."

Nick pulled a face. "Tenuous at best. Coffs Harbour has a population of what, around seventy thousand?"

"I have no idea, only that it's much bigger than Port Macquarie, and Port Macquarie has a population of around fifty thousand."

The two men exchanged glances. "Kevin Hegarty also comes from Coffs Harbour," Nick said, "but then again, it *is* a big place."

"Then he has to be a suspect too," I said. "He did say they weren't friends, but I wonder if they knew each other?"

"I did see Rufus and Kevin at a meeting only recently," Atticus told me. "Of course, Rufus might have been hiding from Kevin. I didn't see them together."

I was certain my face had fallen. "That's a shame. I thought we were onto something, with them both being from the same place."

Atticus took up the story there. "Lots of people move to the mountain from the Port Macquarie and Coffs Harbour areas," he told me. "It's a similar climate, I suppose, although better here."

"I see. Now it's my turn to question you. Could you please tell me about Rufus poisoning your plants?"

An unmistakable look of anger flashed across both their faces. "Rufus moved next door to us a year ago," Atticus said. "We had lots of plants along the border—jasmine, jacaranda, bougainvillea, wisteria. We also had a whole line of established bamboo along the border, for screening. It was the clumping bamboo, not the invasive bamboo that spreads."

Nick took up the story. "Anyway, the last people who owned the place had it on the market for some time. They'd already left for their new place in far north Queensland, so nobody looked after the gardens. When Rufus came, it was overgrown, so he poisoned everything."

"He poisoned all the plants along the border, even the tall established bamboo plants and all the mock orange shrubs," Atticus added.

"So, he didn't want privacy?" I asked, somewhat puzzled.

"Who knows?" Nick threw up both hands to the ceiling. "Anyway, we went to speak to him about the poison, but he became enraged."

Atticus butted in. "The day he moved in, we went over to introduce ourselves, and we were very nice to him, weren't we, Nick!"

"Yes, we were very nice indeed."

"We had a greenhouse with our prize orchids and bromeliads down the back of our place, on the side near his house. One day, we went in, and all the plants were dead. He poisoned them all."

"With fast acting poison," Atticus added.

"Did you go to the police?"

Nick nodded. "Yes, but that seems to be working against us now. The police spoke to him, but he denied it. He said he'd been poisoning out the back of his place and the wind must have carried the poison, but obviously that wasn't true.

After that, we went to the expense of having a front fence built with a big, electronically-controlled gate."

Atticus meanwhile had selected himself a coffee and a cupcake. He had just finished the cupcake. "And we got a security system as well. Not one of those ones that cost thousands of dollars, mind you, just one we bought from an electrical store."

"We bought a set on sale that came with four cameras, so we actually bought two sets," Nick said. "That way we'll know if he ever tries to come onto our property again." He slapped himself on the side of the head. "Goodness me! He's dead, and I'm speaking as though he's still alive."

I felt sorry for them. "That's terrible. So, you have been living here for years, and you lived next door to him for a whole year. Do you have any idea who'd want to kill him?"

"As much as it pains me to say it, Atticus and I had a motive," Nick admitted. "Most of the people in town probably wanted to kill him, and his son had the most to gain. Did you see the cheap coffin?"

Delilah appeared at my side. "Yes, my sister

and I knew it was a very cheap coffin," she said. "But doesn't he inherit a lot?"

"Yes, quite a lot but he doesn't inherit it yet," Atticus pointed out. "He will have to wait for probate to come through, and that could take months."

Delilah shook her head. "But when somebody dies, the bank will release funds to pay for all the funeral expenses."

Atticus shrugged. "So maybe he wants to keep it all for himself. I don't know how much he makes as a golf professional, but I thought they made good money. Perhaps he has a gambling problem."

Nick chuckled. "Oh Atticus, sometimes your imagination does run away with you."

Atticus was not to be put off. "You know, I think I'm onto something. Maybe he *does* have a gambling addiction, and that's why he wanted to kill him."

Now I was lost. "Who wanted to kill him?"

Atticus waved one finger at me. "Well then, that's the six million question, isn't it! Maybe the Brisbane mafia wanted to kill him. Maybe he owed them a lot of money and wouldn't pay out."

I gasped. "There's a Brisbane mafia?"

Nick chuckled. "Of course there isn't. Pay Atticus no mind. He watches too much TV, and as I said, his imagination runs away with him." He addressed Delilah. "Are you and your sister assisting Nell here in her investigation?"

Delilah narrowed her eyes. "So, the cat's out of the bag, is it?" she asked me.

"I'm afraid it is."

"Then yes, we *are* helping her. Do you have any idea who did it?"

"Plenty of people disliked Rufus," Atticus said, "but feeling like you want to do away with someone and actually doing it are two completely different things. His son had the most to gain. Anyway, Nell, why don't you come and visit us? We can have a cup of tea, and we can welcome you to the community. "

"Thanks, that would be nice," I said.

The two of them walked away, in the direction of a cheese platter.

Delilah grabbed my arm. "You shouldn't have agreed!" she said urgently.

I was perplexed. "Why not?"

"Because I'm fairly certain those two are the murderers! And now they know you're investigating, you will be next on their list."

CHAPTER 18

I decided not to visit Nick and Atticus, not on my own anyway. Maybe I *should* leave it up to the police, after all. They hadn't taken me in for questioning again, and they seemed to have lost interest in me as a suspect. I hoped that was the case.

I spent a pleasant afternoon with customers. I was passionate about books and enjoyed chatting with the customers about them. I knew about recent releases and the general book world such as genre fiction and literary fiction, even the classics, but I needed Edison to advise on the uncommon or technical volumes.

I was beginning to think I might enjoy my life

in Wild Lime Mountain. I liked nothing better than being surrounded by books. I waved the last customer out of the door at closing time and smiled.

Edison clapped his hands. "Your first successful day."

"It wasn't a whole day because of the funeral," I reminded him.

He shook his head. "A successful day, nevertheless. I put a bottle of champagne in your fridge for this occasion."

I rubbed my hands with glee. "Thanks so much, Edison."

"Go into your living room, and I'll bring in the champagne."

I didn't need telling twice. I walked into the living room, took off my shoes, put my feet up on the ottoman, and leant back in the chair.

"I want champagne too," said a voice coming from floor level.

I looked down to see JenniFur staring up at me. "Cats don't drink champagne," I told her.

"Who makes the rules?" she said. "Cats don't speak either."

Edison walked into the room holding two

champagne flutes. "JenniFur would like some champagne too," I told him.

He looked shocked but simply said, "Okay."

"And not in a saucer," JenniFur called out after him. "I want a champagne flute too."

I wondered why she looked back at me expectantly, and then I realised that Edison couldn't hear her. "JenniFur wants a champagne flute too please, Edison." I thought about it some more. To JenniFur, I said, "Maybe a wine glass? It will be hard for you to lap out of the champagne flute."

JenniFur looked quite put out. "Then a crystal wine glass instead." She opened her eyes wide and fixed me with a glare.

"Make that a crystal wine glass for JenniFur please, Edison," I called out loudly. I thought it impolite to yell, but I really didn't want to get out of my chair. It had been a long day, and my feet were tired.

Edison presently returned with two champagne flutes and the crystal wine glass for JenniFur. It was filled to the brim. He handed me a champagne flute, placed one on the little cedar table beside his chair, and then placed the full crystal wine glass on top of the tiles around the fireplace.

"Thank you," JenniFur said before she lapped up the champagne.

"Careful," I admonished her. "You don't want to get drunk. How would we explain a drunk cat to somebody?"

She ignored me and continued to lap the champagne.

We made a toast. I thought JenniFur would be put out not to join in, but she was still lapping her champagne. "This is the life," I said Edison.

A knock on the door startled me. Edison and I exchanged glances. I got up and walked over to the door, making sure I looked out the window first. My stomach sank. It was Detective Cole, and given that it was after hours, I was certain he didn't want to buy a book.

I tried not to look too displeased when I opened the door.

"Ms Darling, may I come in?"

I stood aside and waved him in.

The detective did not look at all happy to see Edison. "May I speak with you in private?"

Edison stood up and picked up his

champagne. "I'll wait in the kitchen for you, Nell."

I afforded him a brief nod.

As soon as Edison left, Detective Cole turned his attention to the cat.

"Should the cat be drinking champagne?"

"It's water," I lied. "What can I do for you, Detective? You obviously haven't caught the killer yet."

"I simply want to ask you some more questions, to fill in the pieces, so to speak. Please tell me the circumstances surrounding your purchase of the shop."

My jaw fell open. "The shop? How can that possibly be relevant? Why would you want to know that?"

He narrowed his eyes. "Please answer the question, Ms Darling. And in as much detail as possible, please. Go over the events that led to you purchasing the shop."

I thought his question rather strange. I took another sip of champagne before answering. "Well, let me see." My mind suddenly went blank, and I had a paranoid thought that the detective might suspect I was stalling for time. I took a deep breath and tried to gather my wits. "My divorce recently came through, as I already told you."

I broke off to glare at him before pushing on. "I had no intention of buying a bookshop or moving interstate, but I wanted a change. I saw a movie about a woman who wanted a change, so she moved to Italy and bought a villa."

"So, you intended to move to Italy and buy a villa?"

"No!" I snapped. "That was a metaphor for starting a new life. After I saw the movie, I was inspired to get out of my comfort zone and do something entirely different. Anyway, I went to a fair and there was a fortune teller."

I paused for a breath, but he waved one hand at me. "Please go on."

"She gave me a reading and told me I was going to buy a bookshop in Wild Lime Mountain. She said when the opportunity came up, I should take it, and my life would completely change."

I expected him to tell me to continue, but he seemed fixated on the fortune teller. "How did you meet this fortune teller?"

"I told you. I went to a fair, and she happened to be there."

He shook his head. "No, I mean did you go

into her tent—I assume there was a tent?" Without waiting for an answer, he continued. "My question is, did you go into her tent or her place of business, or did she solicit your business? That is, were you walking through the fair and she came out and offered to give you a reading?"

"Yes, that's exactly what happened," I said. "I was walking near her tent—yes, it was a tent—and she came out and offered me a reading. But what does this have to do with anything? This can't possibly have anything to do with the murder?"

He did not answer me but countered my question with a question. "What was her name?"

I tried to recall. "Madam, um, I forget. I think it was Madam something. That wasn't her real name, of course."

"Could you describe her to me?"

I frowned deeply and then immediately ran my hands over my face to smooth out the wrinkles. I was afraid of plastic surgery and all cosmetic treatments that involved any sort of pain, so I had been watching face yoga on YouTube tutorials. The instructor always warned people not to frown. I looked up to see the detective waiting impatiently.

"Oh, her description? Well, I think she was about fifty, give or take. She had black wavy hair, and I think she had blue or green eyes, but I can't be sure. She was wearing a lot of make-up. She was of a medium build, and she was a little taller than I am." I stood up and held my hand a little above my head. "I didn't see her shoes. I was wearing flats, so maybe she was only taller because she was wearing heels. *If* she was wearing heels," I added. "Is she a suspect in the murder?"

Before he could answer, I said, "Because why would she tell me to buy the bookshop just so she could drive all the way to Queensland to lure Rufus in here and murder him? It makes absolutely no sense. And how would she know I'd buy the bookshop?"

"And how *did* you buy the bookshop?"

"When I went home, I looked on the Internet for businesses for sale in Wild Lime Mountain, and I found the bookshop. I thought it was meant to be, so I emailed the owner."

"You emailed the real estate agent?"

I shook my head. "No, it wasn't on one of the main real estate sites. It was on a For Sale by Owner website."

"And may I see the sales contract?"

What a strange request. I stood up. "I'll go and fetch it." As I left the room, I looked behind me to see JenniFur had consumed the whole glass of champagne. I hoped it wouldn't affect her in any way.

I went up to my bedroom and looked through my bottom drawer which served as my filing cabinet. I had thrown a whole bunch of receipts in there. I made a mental note to get all my paperwork sorted out in a hurry.

I walked back into the room with the document in hand just in time to see JenniFur jump up onto the detective's lap. She missed and fell on her back, her paws in the air. A strange sound came out of her throat, something like giggling.

"What's that strange sound?" Detective Cole said.

"It's the cat. Can you hear it?"

He looked surprised. "Of course, I can hear it. Is the cat all right?"

"She's drunk," I admitted. "Maybe there was champagne in that glass instead of water, after all."

I could see he didn't believe me and knew I had given the cat champagne. He *was* a detective, after all. Thankfully, he did not comment but held out his hand for the contract. He read through it and then made notes.

A horrible sound overhead made us both jump. JenniFur was hanging from the chandelier above us by her back feet and was swinging. I jumped up and reached for her. "JenniFur, get down right now!"

She swiped at me with her paws.

I turned to the detective. "Is that all for now? I have a situation here. I will have to get Edison to help me."

The detective stood too. He walked over to me and stood a little too close for comfort. The energy was palpable. "That's all for now, Ms Darling. Thank you for your co-operation. I will be in touch."

With that, he strode out of the door. I ran after him and locked behind him and then called out, "Edison!"

Edison hurried into the room and gasped when he saw JenniFur hanging from the chandelier. "She's drunk," I said, somewhat unnecessarily.

"I'll get her down with cat treats," Edison said.

"Should she be eating when she's so drunk?"

Edison scratched his head. "Maybe not. We'll leave her there for a minute. What did the detective want?"

I filled him in on the detective's strange request.

Edison appeared perturbed. "How strange! Well, never mind. I'll fetch us some more champagne. No more for JenniFur, of course."

With that, he hurried out of the room.

JenniFur detached herself from the chandelier. She landed softly in a chair and made to follow Edison but tripped over. She got up and shakily trotted out of the room.

I threw myself back in the chair, my pleasant day ruined. Surely this meant I was still a suspect. Why else would the detective be so interested in the circumstances of me buying the shop?

My mind was made up. I would have to question Nick and Atticus. If I made a point of telling them that Edison was minding the shop while I visited them, they were hardly likely to harm me even if they thought I suspected them.

I looked up when I heard a noise, expecting to see Edison return with the champagne. "I want some more," JenniFur said.

"You're drunk," I told her. "No more champagne for you."

JenniFur hiccupped. "Edison is out there calling that fortune teller to warn her the detective is onto her."

CHAPTER 19

"I don't like you going on your own." Edison stopped dusting for a moment, placing his pink and green feather duster on a shelf. "Didn't you say Daphne told you she suspects them?"

"It was Delilah actually, but yes. Still, I told them you were minding the shop for me, so they're hardly likely to harm me when you know I am there."

Edison shook his head and recommenced his dusting.

"They certainly take their plants very seriously," I said. "They told me I was not to cut across the lawn. They said I had to walk down the driveway and then turn left onto the concrete porch. They said they don't allow visitors to contaminate their plants."

"Their garden is quite a tourist attraction, actually. People love to drive past it and look down inside it."

I was intrigued. "What do you mean, look *down* inside it?"

"The road is much higher than their house and garden. They have a concrete fence with an electronically opening gate, the type you see at the Gold Coast, nothing like the picket fences we have here on Wild Lime Mountain. They're extremely proud of their garden. They certainly must be good gardeners because even hail doesn't seem to affect their garden. Why, the cyclone we had last year didn't even damage their plants."

"That's amazing," I said absently. "Do you have any suggestions for what I can ask them?"

Once more, Edison set down the feather duster. "My suggestion is you don't go there at all. It clearly wasn't a local person who killed Rufus. No, it was definitely an outsider, you mark my words. You going there is a complete and utter waste of time."

I rubbed my temples. I had the beginnings of a headache. "It's just that with the detective asking me those questions again, I feel like I have to do something. If he thinks asking bizarre questions about how I met a fortune teller is going to aid in his investigation, then it's quite obvious he won't solve that murder in a million years. And until he solves that murder, I'm going to be on edge."

Edison let out a long sigh. "All right then, if that makes you happy."

"Edison, I almost forgot. JenniFur said you called the fortune teller to warn her Detective Cole was asking questions about her."

Edison's mouth fell open. "How strange. Of course I didn't."

I reached for my handbag from under the counter, but my hand met something furry. I squealed and pulled my hand back.

"Keep it down, will you?" said a voice. "And can you turn off that light? The darker, the better."

I bent down and peered into the shelves under the counter. JenniFur was curled up in a ball. One paw was covering her eyes. "Leave me alone," she said. "I think I'm going to throw up. You should never have let me drink champagne. I am a cat, if you hadn't noticed."

I grabbed my handbag and drew it out slowly so the vibration wouldn't upset JenniFur. "Don't worry, I will never give you champagne again."

JenniFur's paw slipped down her face a little, showing half of one eye. "Well, there's no need to get carried away. That is a little extreme, isn't it?"

I exchanged glances with Edison. "I have my phone in my handbag so call me if you get busy."

Edison chuckled. "The bookstore won't be that busy, trust me. And Nell, they didn't do it."

I didn't know what to say, so I gave him a little wave and made for the door.

Nick and Atticus's house wasn't far away. Nothing was far away on Wild Lime Mountain. I headed for a part of town I hadn't seen before, to the east. As I came over the crest of the hill, I saw the most astounding view of the Gold Coast directly ahead of me, and to my right, spectacular views of mountains. I could have parked there and looked at the view for hours.

As their house was indeed set down from the road, I parked in the driveway. A pedestrian gate next to the main gate opened. I walked inside, and the gate closed behind me, affording me a moment of alarm. I crossed at once to the driveway and then turned left onto the concrete porch as instructed.

Nick greeted me with a wide smile. "Please come inside. Atticus is fussing around in the kitchen." He made a tut-tutting sound with his tongue and rolled his eyes.

The house was entirely crammed with furniture and knickknacks. Most of the furniture was antique, although some was vintage. It was all heavy and of dark wood, absorbing most of the light in the room.

"Come out onto the balcony," Nick said. "Atticus loves this type of thing, but I myself am a minimalist."

I gasped when I walked onto the porch. It offered an expansive view of the Gold Coast skyline and the ocean beyond. "That's Surfers Paradise directly in front of you, and to the right you can see as far as Coolangatta, to the Gold Coast Airport," Nick told me.

Atticus appeared as if from nowhere. "How lovely to see you, Nell. Do you like our view?"

"I love your view," I told him. "I wish I had a view like that. I do have a view of lovely tropical trees, and at night the rosellas and the sulphur crested cockatoos land on them."

"It's always nice to have a view of something." Nick nodded slowly.

"How do you have your coffee?" Atticus asked me. "Or would you prefer a cup of tea?"

"Or maybe some wine?" Nick asked.

"Coffee would be lovely, please. Black, with two sugars."

I sat, admiring the view. Atticus presently returned with a large tray on which were perched three cups and a French press. He set the French press in the centre of the table along with a bowl of sugar and set a cup in front of each of us. He also set a plate of cupcakes on the table. "Do you like cupcakes?" he asked me.

"I love cupcakes," I admitted.

"I'll bet your favourite book when you were a child was Enid Blyton's *The Magic Faraway Tree*," Nick said. "And I'm sure part of the reason you love the book was the lovely descriptions of food."

My hand flew to my throat. "But, but how did you know?" I asked.

Atticus glared at Nick. "Nick fancies himself as a bit of a psychic," he said through narrowed eyes.

"Pish posh. I *am* a psychic," Nick said rather

crossly. "And am I right?" He threw up both hands, palms to the ceiling.

"You're absolutely right," I said. "I remember the sherbet-filled buns, the Pop Cakes, the Toffee Shock cake." Nostalgia overwhelmed me, but then I turned my attention to the investigation. "But are you joking or are you really psychic? Do you know who the murderer is?"

Nick sighed and then put his head in his hands. After a moment, he took his hands away and looked at me. "I'm afraid it doesn't work like that. I'm not psychic on demand, you see. Things just come to me out of the blue, and there's absolutely no rhyme or reason to it. If somebody wanted me to answer a question for them, I would not be able to do so."

Atticus sat down hard. "Yes, that's true. But please don't tell anybody. People have asked Nick all sorts of questions, and when he doesn't answer them, they think he's withholding information. But what he says is true. He gets flashes of well, I suppose what you would call knowledge, and it's completely at random. That's why he doesn't know who the murderer is."

"That's exactly how it is," Nick added. "The other day I was in the supermarket, and Mrs

Jones was there. Do you know Mrs Jones? She works in one of the pottery shops in town."

"No, I don't know her," I said.

"Well, the other day at the supermarket, I told her that her husband was having an affair but that she would win a substantial amount on the lottery the following week."

"And did she?"

He nodded. "And the good thing was, she left her husband the day before. I don't think he even knows about the lottery money."

We were digressing somewhat from the murder. "One of the detectives came to see me just after closing yesterday afternoon," I told them. "I thought I was no longer a suspect, but it seems as though I am."

"Was he asking you about your motive?" Atticus asked me.

I shook my head. I considered the matter, but I could see no harm in telling them. "No, it was the strangest thing. He asked me how I came to buy the shop on Wild Lime Mountain."

The two men exchanged glances. "Was that all he asked?" Atticus asked me.

"Yes, he gave me the third degree about it, but I couldn't see how it's relevant at all. Anyway, it unnerved me, and it prompted me to try to do some investigating myself."

"But it might not be safe for you." Nick's face turned a ghastly shade of red.

Was he threatening me? I couldn't be sure. "Nick, have the police questioned you again?"

"No, the last time we saw the police was at the funeral yesterday, and they didn't question us there," Atticus told me. "Have you met Kevin Hegarty? He was at the funeral. We spoke about him, remember?"

"Yes, I met him at the Welcome to Wild Lime Mountain meeting the other evening," I told them. "Do you suspect him?"

Nick tapped his chin. "I do find it a little suspicious that he was at the funeral. After all, he said he didn't know Rufus."

"He told me he was trying to socialise, you know, to make friends," I told them.

Nick stood up. "Just a moment."

I had eaten a whole lemon iced cupcake by the time he returned. He slapped an A4 sheet of paper in front of me. "Kevin Hegarty said he hadn't met Rufus, but look at this." He jabbed his finger on the photo.

I leant forward. "I don't think I've brought my

glasses."

Atticus ripped his glasses off his face. "Here, try mine."

I popped them on and bent over the photo. "This certainly looks like Kevin, and Rufus too, although I only ever saw Rufus once, when he was alive, that is. I can't be sure. This seems to be an old photo. Where did you find it?"

"Atticus and I were doing some investigating of our own," Nick told me. "Last night we spent hours on the Internet researching Rufus. We were looking at old photos of him and..." He would have said more, but I interrupted him.

"But how did you? Didn't he change his name?"

"Oh yes, his old name was Gary Greaves."

I was quite surprised. "But how did you know that?"

"Oh, everyone in town knows," Atticus said.

Nick chuckled. "Actually, *everybody* in town doesn't know that, but we know. We were friends with the real estate agent who sold him the house. That is, the agent who sold him his first house when he moved to the mountain. It's all supposed to be hush-hush, you see. Oh well, now that he's dead, it won't matter if it gets out."

"I suppose not. Go on, so you researched his real name, and you found these photos?"

"Yes, and it's very strange that Kevin Hegarty obviously knew Rufus, although he alleges that he didn't."

I thought it over. "And Kevin Hegarty only moved to town two months ago. That makes sense."

Atticus leant over the table. "I'm not following. What makes sense?"

"It makes sense that Kevin could be the murderer. He moved to town two months ago, recognised Rufus, and decided to kill him. He must've had an old grudge against him. Now that photo you found on the Internet—were they playing in a soccer team together?"

Nick nodded. "Yes, it looks as though they did. And before you ask, yes, I have searched on the Internet for both their names together, but nothing has come up."

"It proves Kevin is lying, though," I said. "He said he'd never met Rufus before. Why would he lie about something like that, unless he had something to hide?"

Both men nodded. "Precisely," they both said in unison.

"Are you going to show that photo to the police?"

They both continued to nod. "We already have," Atticus said. "We showed it to Detective Stevens."

"Can I take a photo of it?"

Nick said that I could, so I wasted no time pulling out my phone. "I hope they investigate Kevin." I took a bite, this time of a Black Forest cupcake. "Wow, this is delicious. Did you make it yourself?"

Atticus smiled, but the look was fleeting. "We also found out something else, but we didn't tell the police."

"Why not?"

"Because Detective Stevens's attitude was that we're trying to throw suspicion off ourselves."

Nick agreed with Atticus. "Yes, he did give that distinct impression. That's why we didn't want to give him any further information."

"You have more incriminating evidence against Kevin Hegarty?"

Nick rubbed his hand over his eyes before sighing. He took a deep breath and let it out slowly. "Yes, but we don't know how it ties in. You know, of course, that Rufus's wife was murdered ten years ago?" I nodded. He pushed on. "There was an attempt on the life of Kevin Hegarty's wife in the very same week."

"You're kidding!"

Both men shook their heads slowly. Nick was the first to speak. "Maybe Kevin is a serial killer and went on a killing spree. The attempt on his wife failed, so he got angry and killed somebody else's wife who just happened to be Rufus's wife."

I thought that a little far-fetched but didn't like to say so.

Nick must have noticed my hesitation, as he pushed on in overly enthusiastic tones. "Don't you see? Both men knew each other, and now Kevin is saying he didn't know Rufus. That is suspicious in itself. And what are the odds of two men's wives being murdered in the same week?"

"Oh, was Kevin's wife murdered? I thought you said it was an attempted murder." I was perplexed.

Atticus patted Nick on the shoulder. "What Nick meant to say was that it was strange that the two men knew each other. One wife was murdered, and the other wife was nearly murdered in the same week."

"Was that a burglary gone wrong too?" I

asked. "I don't suppose she got a look at her attacker?"

Nick shook his head. "Somebody shot at her. Apparently, she arrived home and was carrying her grocery shopping from her car into her house. Somebody shot at her and missed, shooting her car window instead."

"Was it close?" I asked.

"Yes, very close," Nick said. "It missed her by this much." He held up his thumb and finger to show me the distance.

"Wow." I couldn't think of anything else to say.

Atticus chipped in. "And they never found the weapon."

"But they would have known what sort of gun it was," I said.

"Yes. Oh, I've gone blank, but it was a common rifle, the type used for shooting snakes on a farm. Illegally, of course."

Atticus agreed with Nick. "And Rufus used to live on a farm. He's such an unpleasant person. Perhaps he annoyed another farmer."

Nick's face once more flashed red. "No, no, no, Atticus. You're getting all mixed up. Rufus's wife wasn't shot with a rifle, it was Kevin's wife who was nearly shot with a rifle."

Atticus appeared quite put out. "I am not mixed up at all. Rufus and Kevin knew each other, so they probably had friends in common."

"But you said Rufus might have annoyed another farmer."

Atticus scratched his head. "You're right. I'm completely confused."

"It *is* rather confusing," Nick admitted, "but I am certain Kevin Hegarty is the killer."

CHAPTER 20

I decided I had to speak to Kevin Hegarty. I had no idea where to find him, and I didn't want to go to another golf course. I still had a bad case of sunburn from the other day.

I called Edison to make sure he didn't need help at the shop, and he assured me that he didn't. He told me Kevin Hegarty often had lunch at a café in Lamington Lane, although he couldn't tell me which one.

I pulled into my parking spot at the bookstore and thought I should check in with Edison in person.

He looked up in surprise to see me. "I thought you were going in search of Kevin Hegarty?"

"I am, but I'm going to walk down Lamington Lane and look in all the cafés," I told him.

"Why do you want to speak to him? Was it something Nick and Atticus said?"

"Yes, they think he did it."

Edison smiled and nodded. "Well, I'm glad you no longer think it was Nick and Atticus." He narrowed his eyes. "Or do you?"

I shook my head. "No, I'm beginning to agree with them that it was Kevin Hegarty. Did you know there was an attempt on his wife's life the same week that Rufus's wife was murdered?"

Edison gasped. "I had no idea. But why would that implicate Kevin? Would he have a reason for killing his own wife as well as Rufus's wife?"

I scratched my head. "I haven't figured out that part yet, but the timing seems way too much of a coincidence. Maybe the wives were good friends with each other and were blackmailing Kevin about something."

JenniFur appeared and meowed loudly. "Then if Kevin is the murderer, you should stay away from him. Leave it to the police. Why don't you call that handsome detective and tell him the information?"

"I will speak to Kevin first and then tell the

detective what I find out," I told her. "I should get some information first, or he'll say what Edison said, namely, he'll ask what possible motive could Kevin have."

"Then tell him he can't expect you to solve the case for him," JenniFur said. "You're attracted to him, I know, and he's attracted to you. Cats know these things. How will he ask you out on a date if he doesn't see you again?"

I felt my cheeks turn hot, and it wasn't from a hot flash this time.

"What is JenniFur saying?" Edison asked me.

"She says I should tell the detective."

Edison raised his eyebrows but didn't say anything else.

"Since there are no customers, I'll walk down the street and see if I can find Kevin."

The air was hot and cloying, worsened by the lack of any breeze. Port Macquarie had been humid, but the Queensland humidity was something else. Plus, up on the mountain, there were no refreshing sea breezes.

After walking for some time, I reached the end of Lamington Lane and crossed the road to walk back along the other side. I spotted Detective Cole walking where I had just been.

Still, he was a local, so maybe it didn't mean anything.

I kept walking in search of Kevin. I had almost given up hope when I saw him sitting at a wooden table under a giant shade sail cloth out the front of one of the cafés. I walked inside and ordered a coffee. The barista said she would bring it to my table.

I walked over to Kevin. "Can I join you?"

He looked up and smiled. "Certainly."

I decided to come straight to the point rather than beating around the bush. "The police are still suspicious of me."

He appeared startled. "What? They think you killed that man?"

I nodded. "Yes, and just between us, I've decided to do some investigating. I hope you can help me."

Kevin pushed his plate away. Half an egg and lettuce sandwich was still sitting on it. "How can I possibly be of help?"

I selected the photos on my phone and showed him the photo of him with Rufus. "Do you remember this photo?"

He stared at the photo and then smiled. "Yes, I used to play soccer before I hurt my knee." He looked up and scratched the back of his neck. "But what does this have to do with Rufus Rutherford?"

"That's him there." I jabbed my finger on Rufus's photo.

Kevin frowned. He held out his hand for my phone and then widened his eyes. "No, that's not Rufus Rutherford," he said. "That's Gary Greaves. I'm sure of it."

I shook my head and then nodded. "Rufus Rutherford *is* Gary Greaves, or rather, he was. He changed his name when he came to Wild Lime Mountain."

Kevin was visibly taken aback. "But are you sure? Why would he do that?"

"His wife was murdered ten years ago, and he didn't want people to ask him questions about it. Apparently, it was big news at the time."

Kevin nodded vigorously. "Yes, it was. I wasn't still in touch with him by then, but I did see it on the news. That poor man. I didn't know him at all. I only played soccer with him. He wasn't a nice person, but you wouldn't want that to happen to anybody."

"Wasn't there was an attempt on your wife's life the same week?"

Kevin gasped. "How do you know that?"

I didn't want to tell him that Nick and Atticus told me, so I said, "Like I said, I'm investigating."

"Yes, but that was a coincidence," he said.

"But it sure seems too much of a coincidence, doesn't it? Was there someone who had it in for both you and Rufus? Or was there a serial killer in town?"

Kevin shook his head. "Rufus's wife was murdered in Coffs Harbour, according to the news reports I saw, but my wife and I were living in Belmont at the time."

"Belmont near Newcastle in New South Wales?"

He shook his head. "No, not that Belmont, the Belmont that's a suburb of Geelong, south of Melbourne."

I was taken aback. That blew my brewing theories out of the water. Geelong and Coffs Harbour were almost two thousand kilometres apart. It wasn't so much of a coincidence, after all.

Kevin continued to nod. He put his head in his hands and groaned. "I hope the police don't find this out because they gave me the third degree back in the day about the attempted shooting of my wife, even though I wasn't even in the state at the time. They certainly were suspicious of me, I can tell you! They questioned me again and again. I couldn't handle any more police questioning." He wiped a tear from his eyes. "Even now if I see a police vehicle on the road, I start shaking."

I could see he was trembling. "Why did the police suspect you of your wife's attempted murder?" I asked him. "Were you good with a rifle or something?"

Kevin sighed again. "No, I've never even held a rifle. No, they were suspicious because she was a very wealthy woman. If something happened to her, I would become a very wealthy man. As it was, our marriage broke up soon after, and I came out of it with nothing. My marriage broke up over that shooting."

"And did the police ever find out who did it?"

He shrugged. "If they did, they never told me. And my ex-wife and I haven't spoken in years. So, if you're asking if somebody had a grudge against me *and* a grudge against Rufus, I think the answer would have to be no. The only enemies I had were my wife and her family. I don't think I've ever upset anybody else badly in my entire life.

And as for Rufus, or Gary as I remember him, he was a thoroughly unpleasant person, but I couldn't tell you if he had any enemies, as I only knew him from the soccer team. I'm sorry I can't be of more help to you."

Back to square one. Kevin had been my Number One Suspect—now what?

Again, an uneasy feeling settled in the pit of my stomach. I saw a familiar pair of shoulders through the Bird of Paradise leaves in front of me. Detective Cole was buying a coffee. He took his coffee to a far table and sat at an angle to me.

It was clear the detective was following me.

CHAPTER 21

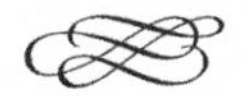

I returned to the shop, somewhat dejected. Who could possibly have a grudge against both Kevin and Rufus? It didn't make sense. It was a coincidence that their wives were attacked in the same week, and it was a coincidence they had both lived in Coffs Harbour and had moved to Wild Lime Mountain, although upon reflection I figured the latter wasn't such a coincidence. After all, at the welcome meeting the other night, I had met a woman who had also come from my old town, Port Macquarie, to Wild Lime Mountain.

When I got back to the bookstore, Edison was serving a customer. I continued on to my apartment to put my handbag upstairs. I was halfway back down the stairs when JenniFur ran past me, nearly tripping me over. "Be careful," I called after her. "These stairs are steep."

She paused and looked over her shoulder. "Not for me," she said. "I must warn you—Edison and the sisters are going to invite you to have dinner with them tonight. It's an intervention." With that, she hissed and ran out of the room.

I was entirely mystified. An intervention? What could I possibly have done wrong? Sure, I had a glass of wine every day, but that was hardly a reason for an intervention. Was it all the cupcakes I had eaten? Too many chocolates? Maybe too much coffee? Perhaps they thought I needed to exercise and drink protein shakes or something. There was no point speculating. I decided I would confront Edison and ask him.

As soon as the customer left, I did just that. "Edison, JenniFur tells me you're going to invite me to have dinner with you, Delilah, and Daphne tonight."

I couldn't be certain, but I thought I saw a look of discomfort pass over his face. "Yes, that's right."

"JenniFur says it's an intervention."

His eyes widened. “An intervention? It certainly is not.”

Still, I knew something was up. I remained silent and looked at him, willing him to speak first. Eventually, he did. “We’re just going to explain to you about the mountain, fill you in on its little quirks.”

I let out a long sigh of relief. “That sounds good, thank you.”

“Dinner will be at Daphne and Delilah’s house, which is directly behind their shop. It has a different entrance. You go down the laneway to the left of the shop, and you will see a blue door. That’s the entrance to their house.”

“That’s awfully kind of them,” I said. “What should I bring?”

“Nothing. They said not to bring anything, just yourself.”

I pursed my lips. Everybody says not to bring anything, but still, a guest would have to bring something. I decided to bring wine or chocolate. “What time?”

“Seven.”

Hours later, at precisely one minute to seven, I was standing on the sisters’ porch, my hand raised to knock on the blue door.

It swung open to reveal Daphne standing there. I judged her too far away from the door to have opened it but dismissed the thought. I held out a bottle of wine. "Thanks so much for inviting me."

Her lips formed a thin line. "Do come in. If you're wondering about the fragrance, it's mugwort. Like sage, only stronger."

I stepped inside the entrance hall. There was indeed a pungent but pleasant fragrance in the air. The entrance hall was white and completely devoid of any decoration—no furniture, no paintings, not even a floor mat—and the walls and tiles were white. I stepped out of the entry and into the living room, and gasped.

It was just like the shop. A line ran down the centre of the room. To my right was a spaceship. That is to say, it was decorated as I would guess an interior of a spaceship would be decorated. I was old enough to have watched the original *Lost in Space* episodes as a child. This room could have been a movie set from that very series.

The room to the right was in a pristine style, although beautifully done, with couches upholstered in a Liberty print and with what appeared to be an expensive Persian rug on the floor. A Tiffany light hung from the ceiling, and it was in stark contrast to the futuristic metallic light in the other side of the room.

Delilah chuckled. "I see you're rather taken aback by our choice in furnishings."

I was about to deny it for the sake of politeness but thought it would be better to be honest. "It is unusual," I admitted.

Daphne shook her head. "As you can see, my sister and I have vastly different tastes in decorating. We couldn't come to an agreement, so we divided up the sections of the house. There are two bedrooms in the house. Clearly, we can decorate our own bedrooms how we like, but the common rooms such as the kitchen and the living room needed to be divided in half. It was the only way we could agree."

"What a good idea," I said.

I hadn't noticed that Edison was already there. He was sitting inside a strange alien styled cubicle. "I do love all this alien stuff," he said with enthusiasm.

"Please come to one of the dining rooms," Daphne said and would have said more, but I spoke first.

"Did you say dining rooms, plural?" I asked her.

She nodded. "This was originally a three-bedroom house when we bought it, but we converted one of the rooms to a dining room. Therefore, one is decorated in my style, and one is decorated in Delilah's,"— she hesitated— "*style*." It was as though she could barely bring herself to say the word. "So, please come into my dining room. I made the dinner while Delilah was working in the shop. I'm going to serve dinner now. There's no point sitting around, making inconsequential small talk about the irrelevancies and microcosms of life, is there? Let's eat."

Edison and I exchanged glances. I followed Daphne into the dining room.

The dining room was beautiful, albeit somewhat old-fashioned. An Australian cedar round table took pride of place in the centre of the room and was surrounded by Australian cedar balloon back chairs of the early Victorian era. I recognised the timber, as Australian cedar has an unmistakable red hue. The chairs were upholstered in the same cherry velvet as the mahogany balloon back chair in my place, and I wondered if they had been done around the same time by a local upholsterer.

A beautiful Victorian Chaise Longue, this one upholstered in a pale pink velvet, sat along the far wall under a huge and ornate gilt mirror. On the opposite wall hung numerous framed Edwardian portraits. I cringed when I looked at them. The people looked awfully stern and were not smiling. I realised that was the norm of the era, but it was disconcerting, nonetheless. I figured they were ancestors of the sisters.

"I hope you like Pinot Noir," Daphne said, but before I could respond, she filled my wine glass. Soon, I was eating a hearty lasagne and nibbling the most delicious garlic bread I had ever eaten.

"Leave room for dessert," Delilah said. "Daphne has made a wonderful lemon meringue pie."

I could scarcely conceal my delight. "That's my favourite," I said. "Edison said you're all going to tell me about Wild Lime Mountain."

I watched as the three of them exchanged glances. Delilah bit her lip; Edison shifted in his seat, and Daphne left the room in a hurry. I started at Edison. "Are you sure this isn't an intervention?"

"Of course not," he said. "We will discuss it after dinner."

Daphne returned to the table and placed a huge lemon meringue pie in the centre. She proceeded to cut it into rather large slices. "Yes, we will speak to you after dinner. Everything seems better on a full stomach."

Little trickles of apprehension ran up my spine. Why did I need to feel better about something? What on earth was going on? I supposed I was about to find out.

After we had eaten the lemon meringue pie, I made to help clear the table, but Daphne would have none of it. "Go and sit with Delilah and Edison, and I'll bring us all some coffee. Would you like some liquor in your coffee?"

"Yes, that would be lovely."

"Baileys?"

I nodded. "Yes, please."

"It will help soothe your nerves," Delilah said, drawing an angry look from her sister.

My stomach clenched. "Why would my nerves need soothing?"

Delilah did not answer but walked into the living room. I followed them in and sat in one of the big, comfortable sofas. I assumed Edison or

Delilah would sit next to me, but the two of them sat opposite.

An uncomfortable silence settled upon us like a heavy cloud. It was a relief when Daphne entered with a tray. The little coffee cups were decorated in pastels and florals and were of a delicate porcelain—I guessed either Ainsley or Tuscan. She handed me a cup and then sat between Edison and Delilah. I thought it did not bode well that the three of them were sitting opposite me. It *did* seem like an intervention, after all.

I sipped my coffee and waited for somebody to speak. My anxiety went into overdrive. Edison was the first to speak. "You probably think it strange that you can hear JenniFur speak to you."

I gasped. "What? Do Daphne and Delilah know?"

"Edison told us," Delilah said as though she were speaking about the weather.

"And you believe me? You believe I can hear a cat speak to me?"

Both sisters nodded. "Of course, dear," Delilah said. "It's only shape shifting, after all, although in JenniFur's case it appears to be permanent."

I could scarcely believe my ears. Had they put some hallucinogenic drug in my coffee? I stared into the cup.

Edison pushed on. "Remember how shocked you were when you realised you could hear JenniFur speaking to you?"

I nodded vigorously.

"What we're about to tell you will come as a shock too. Remember all the fairy tales you heard as a child? The creatures? They are all true."

I drained my coffee in one go. "You've got to be kidding!"

"No, that's what I'm telling you," Edison said.

I shook my head. "I am sorry, but I can't believe that. It's one thing to hear JenniFur talking to me, but I can't believe there are such things about vampires and werewolves."

"What about aliens?" Delilah said hopefully.

Daphne stood up. "Honestly Edison, you have explained it all wrongly." To me, she said, "No, of course we're not talking about vampires and werewolves or any such thing. We are talking about the Faerie."

"The Faerie?" I echoed.

She sat back down. "Yes, the Fae, the Faerie, the Sidhe."

"Yes, I've read about the Fae," I said. "I've read the works about the Faerie by the famous poet, William Butler Yeats, and I've read Lady Gregory's works on the Faerie. I've always been attracted to stories of the Faerie. What does that have to do with anything?"

"It has *everything* to do with everything," Edison said. "You are Faerie."

My hand went to my throat. "What? Are you saying I'm a changeling or something? How can I possibly be Faerie?"

"Tsk tsk." Daphne clicked her tongue. "Allow me to proceed with the explanation, Edison. We mean you come into your powers at menopause. I am sure you are aware that your ancestors were Irish?"

I nodded. "I had my DNA done, and I'm mostly Irish." I was wondering if they were trying to prank me. It was all so surreal.

Daphne gestured to us. "We're all Seelie, of the Summer Court." I opened my mouth to ask a question, but she pushed on. "Most people in Wild Lime Mountain are Seelie of the Summer Court."

"What's the Summer Court?" I asked her.

Edison spoke first. "There are two courts of

the Seelie. In popular fiction, you might have read about them as the Seelie and Unseelie Courts, but with the Seelie in Australia, it is the Summer Court and the Night Court."

"Why not the Summer Court and the Winter Court, or the Day Court and the Night Court?" I asked him.

The three of them laughed uproariously as if I had made the most hilarious joke, but no explanation was forthcoming.

"In Scottish and Irish history, it's all explained a bit differently," Delilah added.

Daphne crossed her arms over her chest. "*I* am the one giving the explanation, if you don't mind." She pursed her lips before continuing. "Of course, normal people come to Wild Lime Mountain as well, but you will discover that most of us here are of the Seelie Court, the Summer Court to be exact."

"By the way, Rufus was not Seelie, but that's how I know Nick and Atticus didn't murder Rufus," Edison told me. "Nick and Atticus are of the Summer Court."

"Unless they're secretly of the Night Court," Daphne added. "Then they possibly *did* murder Rufus."

Edison frowned deeply. I could see they'd had this argument before.

"What powers do you have?" I asked them.

They all looked aghast. "That is not something one discusses in polite company," Daphne said. "Suffice to say, you are coming into your powers now because you have hit that certain time of life, and you can communicate with JenniFur, herself a Seelie."

"But to the point," Edison said, "certain Seelie have certain roles, and you are a Bookmarker. I can tell you I am a Hierophant."

"I thought you weren't going to tell her she was a Bookmarker yet," Daphne snapped.

Edison appeared most put out. "But Nell is taking all this so well. She hasn't had so much as the slightest manifestation of hysteria in response to all this information."

I did, in fact, feel as though I might pass out. Still, I asked, "What is a Bookmarker?"

"A Bookmarker is a Seelie who is a Guardian of Books, obviously," Daphne said, although it was far from obvious to me.

Edison butted in. "Haven't you noticed that you were always attracted to books? No doubt you surrounded yourself with books from a young age, and you have bought a bookshop. You didn't have any furniture delivered, but you had a huge number of books delivered. A Bookmarker is a powerful Guardian of Books."

"You say I have powers? I haven't seen any evidence of them yet, apart from understanding what JenniFur says."

Daphne nodded. "That's because you're just coming to your powers now," she said. "It is about to change."

I remembered something JenniFur had said. It was hard to think while trying to process all this information, all of which sounded bizarre and downright unbelievable. "Edison, JenniFur told me that you called the fortune teller to warn her I had told Detective Cole about her."

Edison's face turned a bright shade of red.

"And you said that wasn't true," I said. "Was it true?"

The red colour continued to the tips of Edison's ears. "Yes, it was true, but I couldn't tell you at the time."

"Do you know the fortune teller?" I asked him.

He shook his head. "No, not personally but I

was able to track her down. She is of the Summer Court also."

This explanation was only serving to make me more confused. "What did that have to do with Detective Cole? Why did you warn her against Detective Cole?"

Their expressions turned grim.

"Because Detective Cole is of the Night Court." Edison's tone was filled with dread.

CHAPTER 22

I'd had a terrible night's sleep. I had tossed and turned all night. Detective Cole was of the Night Court? I didn't even know what that meant, but Edison, Daphne, and Delilah clearly thought that Faerie of the Night Court were to be feared.

They would not give me any information on it even when I pressed them, and I had no idea why. When I asked if Detective Cole could pose a danger to me, they seemed vague about that as well.

As it was a Saturday, there had been tourists everywhere, and I had finished the day exhausted. Even Edison looked tired. After he left, I decided to get my books into some sort of order. I'd had some flatpack bookshelves delivered for the guest bedroom so I could start stacking my books.

JenniFur was asleep when I went to the kitchen for a quick snack. After two cups of coffee and some slices of Vegemite and peanut butter toast, I went upstairs to put the flatpack bookshelves together.

It wasn't as easy as it looked. The instructions seemed to be for a different bookshelf entirely. I finally figured out where all the pieces should go, and then, after an interval, realised I would need a screwdriver.

JenniFur ran into the room. "Where's the fire?" she asked.

"It's the flatpack furniture," I told her.

"That explains the yelling. Why don't you ask that nice detective to do it for you?"

I groaned. "JenniFur, detectives do not assemble flatpack furniture for anybody."

"They do for their girlfriends."

I pulled a face. "I'm *not* his girlfriend. Would you stop trying to be a matchmaker, please?"

JenniFur hissed at me. "No!" With that, she ran out of the room.

I went downstairs and rummaged through the kitchen cupboards, but there was no sign of a screwdriver. Actually, I found two, one far too small and one far too big. I would have to go to the local hardware store. I had seen it when I was on my way to the doctor's clinic, and I knew they were open late.

I was able to find parking easily enough outside. I looked around the shelves and finally found a section with screwdriver bits. The trouble was, there were too many screwdrivers, and I didn't know the size I needed. Still, I would need to have a toolbox in the apartment.

I turned around and nearly bumped into a man, one of the sales assistants. "Are you looking for anything in particular?" he asked me.

"Yes, a screwdriver. "

"A Phillips head or a flat?"

I nodded. "Yes."

He looked at me for a moment and then said, "What do you need a screwdriver for?"

"I'm putting together some flatpack furniture. I assumed all the pieces would be included, but I need a screwdriver. I don't know what type or size, but I thought I should gather some tools. I left all my tools behind. I've only just arrived in town."

He shot me an appraising look. "Oh, so what side of town do you live?"

"Lamington Lane," I told him. "I bought the bookshop with the apartment over it."

His face lit up with recognition. "Oh yes. Do you like living here?"

No, I thought. *I have been accused of murder, discovered I can talk to a cat, and found out I am a Faerie.* Aloud, I said, "Yes, it's lovely." I forced a smile.

He beamed at me. "Maybe you should buy a little toolbox with just the bare essentials in it. That way you'll be certain to have a screwdriver that will fit. Of course, if you buy a single screwdriver and find you need a different size, you're welcome to return and swap it for something else."

"No, I was actually thinking of a toolbox," I told him. "I don't want to spend too much money on one, because I doubt I'll be using it often. Once I put these flat packs together, I doubt I will need tools for anything."

He chuckled. "That's what everybody thinks, but they always come in here for more tools." He beckoned for me to follow him.

We walked past rows of potting mix and rolls of chicken wire and arrived at another section of the shop. In front of me were large gardening implements, and on the shelf below I spotted a toolbox. "That one looks good, but it's a little big for me," I said.

He crouched down and moved the big toolbox aside. Behind it was another toolbox, a small one. He opened the lid and showed me what was inside. He reeled off a list of tools, but I was pleased to see various sizes of screwdrivers. It was also a bargain price. "I'll take it," I said. "Thanks for your help."

"After you pay for it, I'll carry it out to your car for you. You didn't have a pleasant introduction to town, I heard."

I thought for a moment. "Oh yes, Rufus Rutherford yelled at me. That was the very day, in fact the very moment, I arrived in Wild Lime Mountain, so all the yelling came as a horrible shock."

"He wasn't a very nice man," the assistant said in what was clearly a major understatement. "But don't take it personally. For some reason, he seemed to dislike newcomers to town."

I was puzzled. "What do you mean?"

"Only last week, I saw him yelling at another man who hadn't been in town for very long. It was early in the morning, and they were the only ones there. We open at six on weekdays, you see. I do the early shifts and the late shifts here. I'm sure they would have been embarrassed if they'd known I was there watering the seedlings behind the lattice." He gestured in a general direction over his shoulder.

"Rufus Rutherford was yelling at another newcomer to town?" I asked.

He nodded vigorously. "Tearing strips off him, he was! It's a wonder they didn't wake up the whole town. Actually, the other man was yelling louder than Rufus was. I think Rufus picked on the wrong person that time." He broke off and chuckled.

"Did you know who the other man was?"

He stared off at the ceiling. "I can't think of his name, but I'll know it if I hear it. He comes in here a lot. He's redoing his front fence. He's quite handy—used to live on a farm, he said."

My stomach clenched. "Was his name Kevin Hegarty?"

The assistant shot me a blank look. "Could be. I don't know."

I remembered the photo I had on my phone and retrieved my phone from my handbag. I flipped it to the photos and showed him. "Was this him? This would be at least ten years earlier."

"Yes, that's him!" He jabbed his finger on the photo. "And there's Rufus too. Clearly, they had history."

I was gobsmacked. Kevin had said he hadn't seen Rufus since he arrived in Wild Lime Mountain. "Did you hear what they said?"

The assistant shook his head. I waved my card and paid for my purchase. "I'm parked right outside," I told him. He followed me out to my car. I unlocked my door and opened it so we could put the tool box inside.

I thanked him, and as he was turning away, he added, "That's right—the guy was yelling at Rufus for going back on a deal. That's about all I can remember. It was a terrible argument. I thought it would come to blows."

I thanked him and walked around to get into my car. As I did, I looked up, and to my horror, there was Kevin Hegarty bending over one of the wheelbarrows for sale. He was not far away. There was a large Magnolia tree between us, but surely he had heard what we said.

I jumped in my car and hightailed it out of there.

CHAPTER 23

As soon as I got back to the shop, I parked in the usual place and hurried inside. I locked the door behind me and wasted no time searching the shop and the apartment for intruders. I looked under the couches, under my bed, and looked in the cupboards and the wardrobes. I grabbed Detective Cole's card and called him. Maybe he was a dangerous Faerie, but he was also a cop, and I figured I had just solved the murder.

To my dismay, it went straight to message bank. I took a deep breath and launched straight into it. "Detective Cole, this is Nell Darling. I found out Rufus and Kevin Hegarty had a terrible argument outside the hardware store early one morning last week. Kevin accused Rufus of going back on a deal. Call me as soon as you can. I think Kevin killed him."

I hung up. Something else occurred to me. I called him back. "Oh, and I think he knows I'm onto him. I might be in danger."

My battery went flat as I was halfway through the word 'danger,' but I was certain the detective would know what I had intended to say. I had also wanted to call Edison as well as Daphne and Delilah, but now I would have to wait for my phone to charge. It had been running out of battery awfully fast ever since it had performed the latest automatic update. I plugged it in and then contemplated driving somewhere, maybe to the police station. A crack of thunder convinced me otherwise. I certainly didn't want to drive down the mountain in a tropical storm.

I could walk to Daphne and Delilah's home, but what if they weren't there? I didn't want to be out on the street by myself.

I opened the door a crack and looked out onto the street. A chill had descended, turning the formerly hot and humid air icy. Another clap of thunder made me jump. I had heard about the sudden storms in this area and realised that the stories were not exaggerations. Lightning followed soon after, and the next crack of thunder drove me back inside.

I turned around, and the power went out. "My phone!" I said. I thought about plugging my phone into the car to charge it, but I didn't want to go outside and get soaked. Besides, I could hear the unmistakable sound of hail on the tin roof. I locked the door again and went to fetch a book. It was too dark to read printed pages, so I went upstairs to fetch my iPad.

"What's the matter with you?" JenniFur asked me.

"I think I've solved the murder," I told her. "My phone battery's flat and now there's a power outage, but I've left a message for Detective Cole."

"Maybe he'll come to your rescue like a knight in shining armour and sweep you off your feet, then you'll get married and live happily ever after."

"You've been reading too many fairy tales," I said.

"Speaking of the Faerie, did Edison break the news to you that the Detective is a Seelie of the

Night Court? I heard him discussing it with the sisters."

I waved my finger in the air in her direction. "You knew? Why didn't you tell me?"

JenniFur spun around, chasing her tail. I was about to say something else when she finally stopped. "It's not my place to tell you anything. I'm a cat, not a journalist."

"Is there anything else you're keeping from me?" I asked her. "Like, secrets?"

"You're asking the wrong person," she said. "Cats always have secrets."

I rubbed my forehead. "I wish this power would come back on soon."

"Why don't we both have a glass of wine and you can tell me about your murder theory?"

I shook my finger at her. "JenniFur, you can't have any more alcohol. Don't you remember what happened last time?"

"That was champagne. Obviously, cats can't have bubbles. I should be perfectly fine with normal wine."

I shook my head. "You're not having wine. Besides, I shouldn't open the refrigerator door in a power outage."

"You're trying to trick me, but you can't fool a

cat. You have plenty of unopened bottles of wine."

She had me there. "If you promise not to bring up the subject of wine again, I'll tell you about my theory."

JenniFur appeared to be thinking over. She yawned and stretched before speaking. "All right then, tell me. Who did it? Was it the butler?"

"There is no butler."

JenniFur chuckled. Either that or she was coughing up a furball. I pushed on. "It was Kevin Hegarty. I think I have it all figured out now. Of course, I could be wrong, but the pieces all fit."

"Please come to the point," JenniFur said. "You humans can be tedious at times." She yawned widely.

I shrugged. I really could do with a glass of wine, but I didn't want to get one because JenniFur would insist on drinking with me. I launched into my theory. "Kevin Hegarty told everyone he didn't know Rufus Rutherford."

JenniFur held up one paw in the air. "But Rufus Rutherford had changed his name from Gary Greaves."

I waved that comment aside. "Let me finish. Kevin Hegarty and Rufus Rutherford played soccer together when they both lived in Coffs Harbour."

"What? They both lived in Coffs Harbour?" She jumped up onto the mantelpiece and knocked off a fake potted orchid. I dived for it and somehow managed to catch it before it hit the floor.

JenniFur jumped down again. "Well, don't stop there."

"I will tell you what I know for sure, and then I'll tell you the part that's my theory. What I know for sure is that Kevin and Rufus used to play soccer together. Here, I'll show you."

I fetched the photo I had emailed from my phone to my laptop and printed out earlier. It was the image I had photographed at Nick and Atticus's house. "Nick and Atticus found this," I added. "Yet despite Kevin and Rufus being on the same soccer team years ago, Kevin told everybody he didn't know Rufus."

"I see."

"And yesterday, I spoke with Kevin, and he said he hadn't seen Rufus at all since he moved to Wild Lime Mountain. He said he had no idea Rufus was living here because Rufus had changed his name. He said they hadn't been friends, and they were simply on the same soccer team." I paused for breath.

JenniFur waved me on. "Go on. Please get to the interesting part."

"I just went to the hardware store. The man there told me he saw Rufus and Kevin having a terrible argument just outside the store one day last week. It was early morning. Nobody else was around, and he didn't think they saw him."

"But Rufus yelled at everybody. He had a terrible temper."

I shook my head. "But don't you see? Kevin said he didn't know Rufus, but he was screaming at him in the street. He accused Rufus of backing out on a deal."

JenniFur's paw went to her mouth. "Curiouser and curiouser."

"That's the end of the facts as I know them, and here is the beginning of my theory," I continued. "Rufus and Kevin had both married very wealthy women. Rufus's wife was murdered, and he had an excellent, iron clad alibi. There was an attempt on the life of Kevin's wife in that very same week."

JenniFur hopped up onto the coffee table.

"And you're about to tell me that wasn't a coincidence?"

"That wasn't a coincidence at all," I agreed. "If my theory is correct, both men made a deal with each other that they would kill each other's wives. Kevin killed Rufus's wife first. Rufus was hundreds of kilometres away at the time and was seen by everybody at a conference. Then a few days later, I am guessing that Rufus flew to Melbourne, no doubt hired a car, drove to Geelong and shot at Kevin's wife. However, he missed."

"Why didn't he make another attempt?" JenniFur asked me.

I shrugged. "Who knows? But the thing was, Kevin also had a very good alibi at the time because he was visiting his parents at their farm near Adelaide. He was also seen by plenty of people at the time his wife was nearly shot."

JenniFur nodded slowly. "I see. So, by making the deal to kill each other's wives, they were able to establish iron clad alibis. The police would never suspect them."

"That's right." The driving rain was making the air chillier by the minute. I contemplated lighting the fire. "And that is why Kevin murdered Rufus, because Rufus backed out of the deal."

"I thought you were wrong at first, but now you've explained it all, I think you're right," JenniFur said. "That's why Kevin yelled at Rufus and said he'd backed out of the deal."

I nodded. "And that is precisely why Rufus changed his name. I mean, Kevin must have been absolutely furious. He had murdered Rufus's wife. Everyone in town said that Rufus's wife's death left Rufus very wealthy. Rufus would have been the prime suspect, only he was attending the conference in Sydney at the time and was seen by heaps of people. Yet instead of going through with the deal and murdering Kevin's wife, he made an attempt and didn't follow through. That left Kevin broke. When Kevin discovered Rufus was here on Wild Lime Mountain, he would have become enraged."

I heard a noise, and then somebody stepped out of the shadows. "You're right. I sure was furious," Kevin said.

CHAPTER 24

Everything stilled around me. "Kevin." My voice was little more than a croak. "How did you get in?"

He snorted. "Obviously, I can pick locks."

"Run!" JenniFur said.

There was nowhere to run. Kevin was blocking my way to the exit.

Kevin took a step towards me. I noticed at once he wasn't holding a gun or a knife. I allowed myself a small moment of relief, but then I remembered how he had murdered Rufus and Rufus's wife.

"I overheard you at the hardware store," he said. "I know you figured it out. Who have you told?"

"The cops," I said. "I called the cops, and they'll be here any minute."

"I watched through the kitchen window when you put your phone on the charger." Kevin's tone was increasingly menacing. "I followed you straight here from the hardware store. Unless you called the cops in your car, I doubt you had time to call anyone. Detective Cole lives on the mountain. He would have been here by now if he wasn't working down at the coast."

I had to buy myself some time. "I understand your motive for murdering Rufus," I said in the calmest tone I could muster, "but what I don't understand, is this. Why did you murder Rufus in my shop? Or why did you murder him and then put him in my shop?"

"To blame you, of course." Kevin held up his hands, palms to the ceiling. "Isn't that obvious? I was trying to lay the blame on you. I saw him screaming at you in the street."

"But nobody murders anybody simply for yelling at them," I said. "Surely, you wouldn't have thought the police would follow that line of thought for too long."

"No," he admitted, "but I thought it would be

a good distraction if only for a short time." He took another step.

"But where did you get the 1080? And how long had you been poisoning him?"

"I used to have a farm, and my parents still do have a farm in Adelaide. A neighbour used to keep his crop dusting plane in my parents' barn, and he had a licence for 1080. It was easy for me to get some, and unless the cops were *really* investigating absolutely every minuscule lead, they'd never be able to link it to me."

"There's one thing I don't understand. I mean, I think I figured it out, but did you and Rufus make a deal to kill each other's wives?"

A smug look covered his face. "Yes, that's exactly what happened." His tone was gleeful, boastful even. "I carried out my side of the bargain, leaving Rufus a very wealthy man. We both made sure we had alibis when the other one was about to commit the murder. It all would have worked, but Rufus missed. How could he miss? Anyway, he didn't follow through, and when I flew back to Coffs Harbour to track him down, he had left town. I tried everything but couldn't find him anywhere. I realised what had happened —he had indeed attempted to murder my wife, but he didn't fulfil his side of the bargain. He chickened out."

"And your wife left you," I said.

He nodded. "My wife suspected I'd put out a hit on her. She told the police as much, but there was no evidence. Because I had signed a prenup, she got everything, and I was left with nothing. I started out as her gardener and pool boy, you see. She was older and a very wealthy woman. I married her for her money, and for years I thought about how she could have a little accident so I could inherit everything and be set up for life."

"What are you going to do?" JenniFur asked me. "You do realise he intends to murder you, don't you?"

"Of course I do," I said.

Kevin appeared puzzled. "What? Anyway, I have to finish you off too." He pulled a pair of plastic gloves out of his pocket and put them on.

"Do something quick!" JenniFur said. "Run! I'll run between his legs and trip him over."

"But there's nowhere to run to." I looked around the room. Kevin was standing in the way of the exit.

"Just accept the inevitable," Kevin said. His

tone was ice-cold. He had murdered two people already.

"You're a powerful Seelie, and he isn't," JenniFur said. "You've hit menopause, haven't you? I've seen you fanning yourself all the time. That's when the Faerie come into our powers. When somebody tried to murder me, I turned myself into a cat."

"I'm not turning myself into a cat," I said. "I wouldn't even know how."

Kevin had finished putting on his gloves. He looked up in surprise.

"Pull yourself together!" JenniFur snapped. "You're a Faerie! You're a Bookmarker! You have magic! He's just a normal person. Do something, Nell. Do something now!"

Kevin picked up the heavy iron fireplace poker and advanced towards me.

I had to think fast. Sure, I was Faerie, but what could I do? What powers did I have? I had no idea, but if I didn't think fast, I would only have moments to live.

"I went into a terrible panic, and that's how I felt my powers bubbling up," JenniFur said. "I went cold all over. Are you going cold all over yet?"

"Yes!" I was surely going cold all over. Panic was overwhelming me in waves. Something indeed was bubbling up inside me.

"Feel the power!" JenniFur encouraged me. "Go with it! Do something to him!"

"But what?"

"Something with a book, I'd guess. You're a Bookmarker."

My eyes fell on the book on the coffee table next to me. It was a heavy, leather bound book, and the cover was gold embossed. Edison must have left it there. I picked it up.

As Kevin brought the poker down on my head, I held up the book to defend myself and recoiled away from the blow.

The blow never landed. I opened my eyes.

There was no sign of Kevin.

It took me a moment to find my voice. "Where is he? Did I send him to another realm? Or did I make him vanish?"

JenniFur's jaw had fallen open. "There were lots of sparks. You used strong magic."

I was exhausted. I sank onto the floor, my back against the chair. I was still holding the book. I looked at it and squealed in horror.

Kevin's face was protruding from the cover, nicely framed by the gold embossing. "Look!"

JenniFur hurried over. "Wow," was all she said.

As we watched, Kevin's face disappeared into the book. The title was replaced with the words, *The Curious Life of Kevin Hegarty*.

The door flew open.

CHAPTER 25

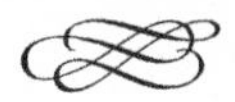

Detective Cole burst into the room. "I got your message and tried to call you back."

"You're too late." I pulled myself up off the floor and into the nearby chair. I resisted the urge to burst into tears. "Kevin was here and tried to kill me."

The detective looked around the room. "Where is he?"

JenniFur meowed. "Good luck explaining that to him!" she added.

"You're trembling. Are you hurt?"

I shook my head. The detective picked up a tartan throw rug from the Chesterfield and wrapped it around my shoulders. His eyes fell on the book. "*The Curious Life of Kevin Hegarty*," he read aloud. "I see." He shot me a long, hard look.

I didn't know what to do.

"Then since the murderer is, err, trapped, do you feel up to telling me what happened?"

I nodded weakly.

"Can I get you a drink?"

"Yes, please," said JenniFur.

"Yes, please," I echoed. "Brandy, wine, anything alcoholic."

Soon, I was sipping wine while the detective busied himself lighting the fire.

"He's as useful as he is handsome." JenniFur purred loudly. "Maybe I should fetch him a rat as a thank you gift."

"No!" I exclaimed.

Detective Cole swung around. "You don't want me to light the fire?"

"Oh yes, please do. I was speaking to the cat."

Edison burst into the room. "Is everyone all right?"

"Kevin tried to murder me."

"Where is he?"

Detective Cole showed him the book. Edison gasped and reached for it. The detective snatched it away and held it to his chest. Edison was clearly none too pleased. "Please give it to me. The book belongs to the bookstore."

"I'll remind you of The Agreements."

Edison narrowed his eyes. "Okay, if you must."

The detective nodded to Edison. "Well then, since the murder has been solved, and the perpetrator has been apprehended, I will be on my way." He walked over to me. "Nell, are you sure you're all right?"

"Yes," I began weakly, but Edison cut me off.

"We'll look after her."

"See that you do." With that, Detective Cole strode from the room.

"What happened?" Edison asked me.

I filled him in with everything that had happened. When I finished, I asked, "But Edison, how did you know something was wrong? I tried to call the detective, but my phone went flat."

"I *am* a Hierophant, remember?"

I shrugged. "I don't know what a Hierophant is or does."

"I felt the powerful surge of magic. That's why I hurried here."

"I see." I didn't really, but I was shaken after the evening's events.

Something occurred to me. "What are The Agreements?"

"The Agreements are hard to explain," Edison said. "But in the context of what happened today, Detective Cole had the right to take that book as evidence. And while it isn't evidence that would stand up in a court of law, the Agreements state that non-Seelie matters take precedence over Seelie matters when it comes to law enforcement. The detective, for the very fact that he *is* a detective, had the right to take the book. Maybe he is concerned Kevin will pop out of it at some time, so he wants to keep it locked up."

That made sense. I was glad something did. "How will Detective Cole explain what happened to Kevin Hegarty?"

"That's his problem," Edison said, none too kindly.

"Humour me. I'm curious."

"He'll figure it out. He would be used to that sort of thing."

"Used to that sort of thing?" I repeated in shock. "He's used to Faerie dealing with non-Faerie murderers?"

Edison shrugged. "He's a capable man. I'm

sure he will come up with a good excuse, and even if he doesn't, nobody will suspect you any longer." He scratched his head. "He'll probably tell the police he discovered that Kevin was the murderer, and everyone will assume Kevin has gone into hiding."

I nodded slowly.

"And I assume Kevin's story is in the book," JenniFur said.

I rubbed my forehead. Only a week ago, I had no idea that I would be having a conversation with a cat or that I was a Seelie of the Summer Court.

There was a loud knock on the door. Edison went to answer it, and Daphne and Delilah tumbled in. Delilah hurried over to me. "Are you all right? Edison said there was a huge surge of power, and he thought it was from you. He took off out of the door like a bat out of hell."

"He was having a cup of tea with us," Daphne explained.

"Kevin Hegarty was the murderer. He came here to try to kill me, and I put him into a book," I said and then wasted no time draining the last of my glass of wine in one gulp.

The sisters appeared shocked. Edison explained what had happened in detail.

"And that Seelie of the Night Court has the book?" Daphne spat.

"The Agreements," Edison said simply.

I spoke up. "I think he's nice."

The other three exchanged glances.

"I think Nell's a little bit drunk," JenniFur said, but of course they couldn't hear her.

Delilah produced a huge box of chocolates. "Times like these call for chocolate," she said. "Edison, don't just stand there. The poor woman needs more wine. On second thoughts, make that champagne."

JenniFur jumped up onto my knee. "Champagne for me too!"

"No, you can never have champagne again," I scolded her.

"But I saved your life," she protested, kneading my legs with her non-retracted claws. "I told you to use your powers."

I sighed. JenniFur was right. She had indeed saved my life. "Please get JenniFur a glass of champagne just this once," I said to Edison. "She helped me find my powers to get rid of Kevin."

That was the last thing I remembered until

I awoke the next morning with a headache. I was still in the living room. The fire had gone out. JenniFur, groaning softly, was lying in front of the fireplace with her paw over her eyes.

"What time is it?" I asked her.

JenniFur's paw moved to cover her ears. "Keep it down, will you? Why did you let me drink all that champagne?"

"You insisted."

"Can you fetch me some sunglasses?"

I stood up and then sat back down abruptly. "I don't feel too well."

"You have a wine hangover and a chocolate hangover," JenniFur informed me.

I stood up again. I fetched a pair of sunglasses from the mantelpiece and put them over JenniFur's face. "Thank you. Edison and the sisters have gone to fetch breakfast."

"They were here all night too?" I asked.

JenniFur looked over the top of her sunglasses briefly to ask, "You don't remember?" She popped back behind her sunglasses.

A knock at the door startled me. "Why didn't they just come in?" I asked JenniFur.

I opened the door and recoiled in horror.

Standing there, on the porch, was my ex-husband.

"Jack!" I said in alarm.

He barrelled past me. "Nell, this nonsense has gone on long enough. You have to come back to Port Macquarie with me."

I was aghast. "What? What about your long-term mistress and your five-year-old child with her?"

"Five years is old enough for it to look after itself," he said.

"You can't be serious!"

He nodded. "Even though you're getting on, and you're not as good looking as you were in your youth, I've decided I will take you back. After all, we shouldn't throw away all those decades we had together."

I folded my arms over my chest. "You drove all this way?"

He shook his head. "I caught a plane to Brisbane Airport and then got an Uber. I've made the decision that you can come back with me. You can put the bookshop up for sale as soon as you get back."

I stomped my foot. "I will do no such thing! You can turn around and take yourself right back where you came from. I never want to see you again. We are divorced, and that's the end of it!"

He shook his head. "I can see that menopause is making you hysterical. Never mind, you can see a good doctor when we go home, and he can give you some pills."

"You can take those pills and shove them right up your *& $!"

JenniFur gasped.

My husband's tone changed to cajoling. "Nell, you can't be serious about this silly little bookshop. You don't have any business sense. You've never been any good with money. Besides, you don't have any friends."

Detective Cole appeared at the door and flashed his badge at Jack. "Is this man harassing you, Nell? Would you like me to lock him up?"

"If he doesn't leave now, that might be a good idea," I said with a smile. "This is my ex-husband, Jack Darling."

Detective Cole was clearly taken aback. He looked Jack up and down.

Edison, Daphne, and Delilah arrived at the door. The detective stepped away.

Delilah was wearing a tinfoil hat and a

transparent, pink plastic raincoat over a bright purple jumpsuit.

"We've brought breakfast," Edison said. "I told JenniFur to tell you we were bringing it."

Delilah held out a plate on which was a large cake. Half of the cake had been shaped into an alien: tall, elongated, and grey, while the other half of the cake had been fashioned into a pretty teacup. It was a work of art—one side of it, at any rate.

"And I've brought more champagne," Edison said. "We have to celebrate you dealing with the murderer."

"Murderer?" Jack shrieked. "What idiocy is this? Nell, at your age! And champagne and cake for breakfast? Who are these people? Are these your new friends? They are obviously a terrible influence on you. This has to end now."

"This is my ex-husband," I explained. "He was just leaving. Jack, go away and don't come back. I never want to see you again."

Jack raised his voice. "Now, listen here..." he boomed, but a heavy hand clamped on his shoulder and spun him around.

"I'm giving you a police escort back to the

airport," Detective Cole said. "And if you ever harass Nell again, you'll have me to deal with."

Detective Cole strode off to his vehicle with my ex-husband trotting lamely beside him.

Delilah clapped her hands. "All's well that ends well," she said. "Let's go inside and eat."

I sat on my comfortable chair by the fireplace, which thankfully had no roaring fire as the weather was now horribly humid again.

I was now confident I would love my life in Queensland. I was surrounded by my new friends: a talking cat, a Hierophant bookshop assistant, and eccentric twin sisters. So much had happened in the last week. I had moved interstate; I had discovered I was a Seelie of the Summer Court; I had solved a murder, and I had thwarted a murderer. And best of all, I had sent my ex-husband packing.

Menopause wasn't so bad after all. I had thought it would be the end of many things, but now I realised it was the beginning of better things to come. And while our society often treated women of my age as has-beens, I smiled as I realised the opposite was true. Women of my age are indeed coming into our power.

THE NEXT BOOK IN THIS SERIES

The next book in this series is
Signs and Pawtents

There have been some fatal accidents in Wild Lime Mountain. The official police position holds there are no suspicious circumstances, but all the victims were of the Summer Court.

With the killer playing cat and mouse, Nell and JenniFur decide to take matters in their own hands—and paws—with the help of Edison, Daphne, and Delilah.

Can they solve the murders? Will there be a pawsitive outcome? Only time will tail.

ABOUT MORGANA BEST

USA Today Bestselling author Morgana Best survived a childhood of deadly spiders and venomous snakes in the Australian outback. Morgana Best writes cozy mysteries and enjoys thinking of delightful new ways to murder her victims.

www.morganabest.com